BLACK LAKE

BLACK LAKE

A Novel

JOHANNA LANE

Little, Brown and Company

New York Boston London

Little, Brown and Company
Hachette Book Group
237 Park Avenue, New York, NY 10017
littlebrown.com

First Edition: May 2014

Little, Brown and Company is a division of Hachette Book Group, Inc. The Little, Brown name and logo are trademarks of Hachette Book Group, Inc.

The publisher is not responsible for websites (or their content) that are not owned by the publisher.

The Hachette Speakers Bureau provides a wide range of authors for speaking events. To find out more, go to hachettespeakersbureau.com or call (866) 376-6591.

ISBN 978-0-316-22883-1
LCCN 2014936485

10 9 8 7 6 5 4 3 2 1

RRD-C

Printed in the United States of America

For my parents

...I regarded men as something much less than the buildings they made and inhabited, as mere lodgers and short-term sub-lessees of small importance in the long, fruitful life of their homes.

—Charles Ryder,
Brideshead Revisited

AUTUMN

When they were little, the door to what was to have been the house's ballroom remained locked. They would stand at the threshold, rattling the handle, first the girl, then the boy, turning it left and right, feeling a split second of give, a moment of hope that this time it might open, but it never did. Their father said that the key was lost, that the room was never finished, that no one had been up there since the house was built. But that was a lie.

When the girl was twelve, her mother plucked her out of boarding school in the city and brought her home. At the door to the ballroom, she slipped a key out of her pocket; the girl's breath caught when it turned easily in the lock. In the vast, secret space, their furniture was doll's house furniture. The mother unpacked the girl's suitcase into a trunk at the foot of the bed, which was covered in a thick eiderdown. She had stolen it from the room below, the room she had shared with the girl's father

3

until the government took over the house and they moved to the small cottage down by the lake.

There was a knock at the door. The girl went to the bottom of the stairs and listened. Her father was on the other side. He whispered her name.

"Dad?"

"Is Mum there?"

The mother arrived, as if she'd glided across the floor. "What is it?"

"What are you doing?" the father asked.

The mother didn't answer.

That night, the mother fell asleep long before the girl. She had driven to the city and back in one day, a ten-hour round-trip. The girl watched her sleep, her lips twitching at the corners every so often as if she were talking to someone in her dreams. There was no electricity in the ballroom, only candles, and though the one next to the bed still burnt, it gave out little light. It was such a contrast to the packed dorms of the boarding school that the girl couldn't help but be afraid. As she lay there, her eyes wandered the darkness, where ghosts of her ancestors could materialize at any moment.

But the next morning was bright and clear. From their warm bed, the girl watched the sun arrive over the sea. The wind was already in the gardens, the tops of the trees bent as if they were straining to talk to each other and straining to hear. The island just beyond the shore was dark, sodden. It had rained during the night. .

That first morning, as the mother slept on, curled up, knees to chin, the girl wondered whether her father would take her for a walk—to look for the deer, perhaps, or to climb up to their favorite place in the hills. She had been at boarding school only a week before her mother took her back. It had been her first time away from home. At night, she had thought about the house, about her old bedroom, about the kitchen, about the gardens, and about the island. Now she understood what "missing" meant.

The tray that was put outside their door half an hour later was the first of many. And, by the end of breakfast, without anything having been said, the girl knew she wasn't going to be allowed downstairs that day. But she couldn't have known that it would be almost a month before she would leave the ballroom at all.

After breakfast, the mother produced a history book, the exact same one the girl had been using at school. They lay on the bed, the sun leaking in the windows. The girl was reading aloud, but she soon sensed that her mother wasn't listening. Before, the girl would have made up something funny, some sort of gobble-degook, so that when her mother realized, she'd laugh and tickle her and make her start again. But the girl knew not to do that sort of thing anymore.

. They did an hour of history. Then, at the girl's insistence, an hour of Irish.

When their lunch arrived, the mother realized that they had no proper table. They'd had their breakfast in bed, but lunch was not a meal to be had in bed, let alone dinner. She could see that the mother was angry with herself for not thinking of this before. "But look," the girl said, and laid out a place mat on each side of the bed, then a knife, a fork, and a napkin. "Clever girl," said the mother, smiling.

When the lunch things had been cleared from outside the door, the mother declared that they needed exercise. They waltzed around and around until the girl was panting more than she had in hockey practice. The floorboards creaked underneath their feet and she imagined falling through to her parents' old room while the guide was in the middle of a tour. She could hear people murmuring below; what would they make of the noises above?

That was the first day. On the second, the father came to the door again, early.

"Is Mum asleep?"

"Yes," the girl whispered back.

"Can you see the key anywhere?"

"It's under her pillow. Haven't you got another?"

"I'm afraid not." An intake of breath. "Don't worry, I'm sure she'll be better soon."

"Will I have to go back to school then?"

"Don't you want to?"

"I don't know," she answered truthfully.

The girl had wanted to go to boarding school. She was tired of having no friends her own age, of having nothing to do, of the endless sea, and of the way her mother had grown strange. But school was all opposites: Where she had had space, now she was confined, where she had sleep, now she woke at the crack of dawn, where she had no friends, now there were too many girls, too much talk.

When the mother came to the girl's history class a few days earlier, her eyes seeking her daughter's, the girl had rejoiced. An afternoon away, perhaps with her grandparents; would they let her curl up and sleep? But the girl and the mother had lunch at a restaurant in town, just the two of them, and after, the mother had swung the car north, away from school, towards the country, towards home. The girl hadn't dared to ask how long she would be back for—or why.

At the beginning, she wasn't afraid in the ballroom. Until the summer, they had been taught at home, mostly by the mother but sometimes, always more interestingly, by the father. The girl was used to settling down to some geography or history or French after breakfast. The mother would leave them work by their cereal bowls and disappear into the gardens, with a promise that she'd return mid-morning.

But soon the days began to run into each other; there was nothing to mark them as different from the ones that went before. They slept, they washed, they ate the meals the housekeeper prepared for them. Boarding school had already accustomed the girl to very little privacy, but using the chamber pot was something she never got used to, though the mother retreated gracefully to the other end of the room when the girl went behind the screen. She learnt to do the same and took solace in the fact that it was removed from outside the door late at night, which suggested that it was the father and not the housekeeper who performed this task.

The girl remembers when the snow began, flakes settling into the windowpanes, muffling everything outside, even the wind. The tourists were gone by then and it was just the sound of her father and the housekeeper moving about below, shutting up the house, covering the beds in dust sheets, rolling up the rugs, storing away quilts no one ever slept under. The girl missed the sound of the visitors, the guide herding them from room to room, story to story. Surely, when the house was finally locked for winter, the father would say that they had to leave, too?

It was after the snow that the mother began to talk about the girl's brother as if he were still with them. One morning, as the girl did her lessons, her mother said, "I'd like you two to have this finished by lunch."

The girl's heart jumped. But it was a tiny word, *two*—a slip of the tongue, perhaps.

Then, a couple of afternoons later, the mother said, as she absentmindedly leafed through a textbook, "Can one of you tell me whether we've done this already?"

From that day onward, the brother joined them for morning classes. He never slept with them, he didn't need the warm water to wash his face in the mornings, he'd no use for the chamber pot, but he was always there for lessons. And the girl came to accept his presence. Or rather, she came to accept that the mother felt him beside them as she stumbled through a sum or conjugated *avoir* and *être*. He was never expected to do any written work, to *produce* anything, and the mother never asked him a direct question, but sometimes, when she asked, "What's the capital of Peru?" or "What's the population of Ireland?" the girl would study the mother's face intently in the silence before she answered, to see whether the mother was listening to him, whether she could hear a faint "Lima" or "The whole of Ireland or just the Republic?" surfacing, drifting in through the window, muffled by the waves.

After the move, the family had lived off a cold roast for days. Her brother had been angry at the chunks of meat that appeared everywhere, in sandwiches, in gravy, or simply, unashamedly cold, with potatoes and carrots, night after night. Now the girl regretted laughing at him when he'd taken a bite and run to the bin to spit it out. He'd opened the desolate fridge and stared into it for a while, as if better food might magically appear if he just stood there long enough. She should have found him something else to eat.

One day, as the snow drifted across the windowpanes, the mother flipped through "Rivers" until she got to "Glaciers."

"I've done that," the girl said gently, careful to say "I" instead of "we."

"But you didn't do it properly, did you?"

The girl looked at her, confused.

"You were too busy swimming this morning, isn't that right? You traced your drawing from the book instead of doing what I asked you to do. Your *younger* brother"—she held up the picture he'd done at the time, which must have been tucked into the pages of the textbook—"did it properly."

The mother was replaying something that had happened almost half a year earlier, the morning after they'd moved out of the big house.

That evening, when the father came to the door, the girl wanted to tell him that she couldn't stay up in the ballroom much longer, that she was ready, now, to go back to school. Perhaps he heard something in her voice, because for the first time he asked if she was all right. What could she say other than yes, forcing herself to sound as if she meant it, as she looked up at her mother standing right there beside her?

One freezing morning, the mother stopped getting out of bed. She turned away, cocooning the duvet more tightly around them, when they heard the housekeeper leave the hot water outside the door.

The girl had become used to the modulation of the father's knocks, usually a soft tap designed not to upset the mother, but sometimes more urgent if he wanted to ask her a question. On this day, when they hadn't eaten their breakfast, then their lunch, he tried calling through the door, first the mother's name, then the girl's. The girl wanted to respond but didn't believe her voice would reach; she felt weak, as if her mother was passing her lethargy on as they lay there. His knocks were loud and firm. One, then another, then again and again. The girl went to the door.

"Enough," was all he said.

Yes, the girl thought, *enough.*

"Can she come to the door?" he asked.

The girl went over to the mother's form, curled like a question mark under the quilt.

"Dad says, 'Enough.'"

The mother stirred. "What?"

The girl repeated the word.

A hum came from the mother, a low hum, like some of the boys in the girl's class did to annoy the teacher, but then the mother's hum turned into something else, something louder, which turned into a sob, and then another and another, until she was gulping in great lungfuls of breath.

The girl ran to the door.

"What's that?"

"It's Mum."

She didn't wait for his answer but went to the bed and curled herself around her mother's back to try to make her stop.

At first, the girl thought he had done what she expected him to do, which was to take away their uneaten lunch, as he had their untouched breakfast. Some minutes passed before she heard the first crash, a crash that sent her knees suddenly into the mother's back so that she shot forwards, her body straightening, her head jerking from the pillow. Someone, it must have been the father—although it seemed impossible to the girl that he was capable of it—was breaking the crockery from their uneaten meal off the door. She could decipher the sharp smash of china and the dull thud of food—an apple, perhaps; then liquid: milk, coffee, soup. And then a more shocking noise, someone crying. A someone she knew was him.

When he had gone, she remained in bed with the mother, long past the point it gave the girl any comfort. It dawned on her that they had been playing a sort of game, a game that had been designed by the mother, yes, but a game that the father had agreed to play, too. That afternoon it became clear that he didn't want to play anymore but didn't know how to stop.

The following morning, the girl managed to get her mother as far as the windows. They watched the wind whip up the waves around the island. The snow had gone, as if it was determined to leave in time for Christmas, as if it was needed elsewhere. The lawn underneath looked damp and sickly.

Someone new came to the door. It was the girl's grandmother, from the city. The mother rose slowly at the sound of her own mother's voice. She approached the door on unsteady legs, and though the girl tried to hear, she couldn't catch everything that the older woman whispered. The mother came back to bed. It was the first time the girl's grandparents had visited since the tourists came, and the girl wondered where they would sleep. There was no space in the cottage for them. Would an exception be made—would they sleep in the house below, in a show bed, under a show bedspread, even though it all belonged to the government now? She imagined her grandparents in their pajamas, returning from the bathroom, having to step over the blue velvet ropes that kept the visitors to one side of the room.

That evening, they ate for the first time in two days and the girl understood it was the bargain that had been struck between her mother and her grandmother. There were tiny envelopes next to their dinner plates, each neatly labeled with their names. The mother opened both. "Vitamins," she muttered under her breath, and handed the girl's to her.

"Why?"

"Your grandmother's very health-conscious."

The girl tried to swallow it with her milk but it was too big and it got caught in her throat. For a moment, she struggled for air. The mother put her hand under the girl's mouth and clapped her on the back, hard. The girl spat out the pill.

"Jee-sus," the mother said.

"I'm sorry, Mum."

She looked her daughter in the eyes, more intently than she'd done in months, and said, "Oh, darling, I didn't mean you. I meant I was angry with *my* mum."

That the girl's grown-up mother could be angry with her more grown-up mother was a revelation.

When it became obvious that the mother wasn't going to come down on her own and that the father didn't have it in him to do what he should, someone—one of the government people, perhaps—phoned the police.

There were so many feet on the stairs that morning that the girl wondered if it was a special winter tour group. When they approached the door to the ballroom, the mother picked up the girl's hand and hid it in her own.

"The guards are here." The father barely got the words out before a soft local voice called through the door.

"I need to speak to"—the guard paused to confirm the girl's name—"Katherine, please, Mrs. Campbell."

The mother sat completely still, her eyes willing the girl to do the same. The girl could feel the heavy weight of the guards' presence; surely the mother would have to give in now?

"I'm obliged to tell you that what you're doing is against the law." It was a man now, harder-voiced.

The mother was still, listening, her head tilted back in defiance.

"I'm all right," the girl called out.

No one answered.

"Am I to understand that it is not your intention to come out, Mrs. Campbell?" he said.

The mother gripped the girl's hand more tightly.

For a while, there was silence outside the door again. The father went to his study to have a last look for a second key; even as he did this he would have known he was stalling. There had only ever been one. It had been in his safe, a safe he thought his wife hadn't known about. When he finally returned to announce that his search had been fruitless, he was very grateful that the house was closed for the winter—that there were no tourists to witness what happened next.

This is the girl's last memory of her mother before she was taken back to Dublin to get better:

They haven't moved from the bed. The mother has her arms

around the girl, covering her ears, muffling the sound of the others' approach. A drill outside, five short bursts, screws falling to the floor. And a sixth, longer this time, the old hinges unwilling to break. The girl wonders if the house is protecting them.

Then a terrible sound, the sound of a crowbar forcing the door open, a deep groan in the wood, and a whoosh of fresh air. The first face the girl sees belongs to the female guard. It contorts in disgust at the stale smell of the room. The others enter slowly. The mother is lifted from the bed by the father. The girl is amazed that he can carry her so easily in his arms, her knees hooked over his elbow, her head resting on his shoulder. The girl takes her grandmother's hand and the guards move in silently behind, touching no one, bringing up the rear. It's as if the whole thing had been choreographed, as if they'd learnt their roles in advance.

Down the never-finished ballroom stairs, the wood rough and splintery; down the main staircase, carpeted now by the government in a lush green; past the stain where the tapestry of the hunt used to hang; and into the hall, the darkest room at Dulough, where the housekeeper and her husband are waiting. Mrs. Connolly opens the front door and Marianne is carried outside, into the watery winter light.

THE SPRING BEFORE

Philip

Dulough faced the Atlantic in the west and backed onto the Poison Glen in the east. It lived by the winds. In the dark, Philip could hear them straining at the windowpanes, trying to force their way in. It was easy to imagine the crash of glass, the furniture tipped over, his clothes whirling about the room like dancing ghosts. He would have slept with the light on if he could, but his father said that it was too expensive.

Fifteen doors opened onto the landing: Philip's, the bathroom, the loo, the upstairs drawing room, his father's study, and nine other bedrooms. His parents' was the biggest, his the smallest. Seven went unused; though there was furniture in each, the beds hadn't been slept in for a long time. His father kept them closed to preserve the heat. When Philip did sneak in, the air was different from that of the lived-in rooms—unbreathed, damp. A final door led to the third floor, but he and his sister weren't allowed up there.

Dulough was a castle, even though it had been built hundreds of years after people stopped building real castles. The house's turrets shot up into the wet sky and a faded pink rose sprawled over the front door. Philip said that the rose looked like the house's mustache. When the blinds in the upstairs rooms were down, the house did have a sleepy, human look about it.

To the west, a waterlogged lawn ran from the front door to the top of the cliffs, which dropped away to the sea. A tall island, not far from the shore, housed a church and the remains of Philip's ancestors; at low tide it could be reached by foot. The lawn was bordered by rhododendrons, the only plant to thrive at Dulough, the only one that needed to be culled each year so as not to swallow up the rest. A kitchen garden had been planted behind the house and beyond that a formal garden. The creation of Philip's mother, a relative newcomer to Donegal, it was a perfect rectangle, with tightly clipped hedges, a paved floor, and a statue dead center. To the east were the hills. They were steep and tall and dark, with ragged grass, and boulders left at precarious angles by a retreating glacier thousands of years earlier. There were waterfalls, too, which began invisibly at the top of the valley and became streams that made fissures in the earth before suddenly disappearing underground again. The red deer lived in the hills, high up in summer but coming down, close to the house, in winter. Though he always watched, Philip could go for weeks without seeing them.

A deep lake bordered the avenue that ran for two miles from the main road, branching off first at the servants' entrance and ending at the front door of the big house. And it was along this avenue that the moving men from Donegal Town came that morning in early April.

*　　*　　*

"Are we taking yourself as well?"

Philip opened his eyes. They stood, their hands already clasped under the iron bed, as if they really would take him with them. The shock of having two strange men in his room made him forget what he had been dreaming about. He hadn't forgotten what day it was, though; they were going to move from the big house to the cottage that had been built for them down by the lake, next door to the Connollys. He sat up, but he didn't want them watching him get out of bed. He was in his pajamas. They wore overalls streaked with dirt. The one who'd spoken to him wore a royal blue fisherman's cap the same color as the overalls. The men were older than his father; they had deep lines in their faces. Like valleys, Philip thought. He imagined tiny glaciers settling into their skin, the ice cracking and expanding. They had been doing glaciated valleys in geography. That was what he had been dreaming about: ice and—

"Up you get there," the man in the cap said. "There's a good lad."

Philip pushed the covers back as the men stared down at his striped pajamas. The man with the deeper wrinkles, the one who hadn't said anything, stood aside for Philip to reach his feet to the floor and put on his slippers. By the time he stood up, they had the bed lifted in the air. Philip made for the door, tying his dressing gown tightly around him as he went. At the threshold, he stopped and turned back to the men, wondering what he should say to them. "Thank you" was what came out, but he was fairly sure it wasn't the right thing.

In the bathroom, Philip looked out the window above the basin. He could see all the way down the valley. It was cold.

When he'd finished brushing his teeth, he said, "Ha"—hard, into the air. His breath came out in a puff, misting the window-pane. Sometimes, in the middle of winter, he and Kate would go for days without having a bath, the thought of stepping from warm water into cold air too much for them. He tried again to remember the dream he'd been having before the men came and took his bed. It was about Dulough and the ice age, but he couldn't remember the details. He looked around the bathroom. Would they come in here? There was nothing for them to take. Everything was bolted to the floor. But he slid the lock over just in case, wondering whether his mother had told the men that they could come into his room while he was still asleep.

The loo flushed next door. It was Kate.

"Did they take your bed?" he asked, letting her in. "They took mine. They woke me up."

"I didn't know they'd come already." Kate sat down on the edge of the bath. "Are you nearly finished?"

Philip looked closely at her. "You've got stuff in your eyes. Here."

He handed her the cloth and she passed it over her face, drops of water catching in her hair. Then he dipped it back in the basin and rubbed it over his own, taking care to delve into the corners of his eyes. It felt nice for one part of his body to be completely warm. Kate gave him a towel.

"Will you get my clothes from my room? They might still be there."

"But I'm not dressed, either."

"Will you just check they're gone then? *Please.*"

He was eight and she was twelve. Sometimes, if he got the tone of his voice right, she would play big sister.

When Kate had given him the all clear, he went back to his room. His bed was gone and there were four rusty indentations on the carpet where the casters had dug in. He put his toe into one of them and twisted it around. His bedside table was gone too, as was the chair where he put his clothes. Only his wardrobe remained: There it stood, towering over the room now that everything else had disappeared. He opened it. Trousers, a shirt, and a jumper lay folded on the bottom shelf. The rest of his things had already been boxed up and taken down to the new cottage at the edge of the lake. He put on his clothes quickly. They were damp. It was always damp in Donegal, even in the middle of summer. Most mornings he draped his clothes over the electric heater in the corner of his room, but there was no time for that today, and besides, the heater was gone. His room looked too big without the furniture to fill it up. The carpet, which was the color of the grass on the tennis court, now looked as big and wide as the tennis court itself.

His room looked out over the back of the house, where hens scratched about in their run and sometimes laid eggs for his breakfast. Further out, at the beginning of the valley, was the barn. It was made of corrugated iron that had long ago begun to rust; sunlight and rain trickled freely through the holes in the walls and roof. It was where Francis kept the winter fodder for the deer and the fertilizer for the gardens. In behind the hay, an ancient Overland car decomposed. When they were younger, Kate and Philip used to sit up in the front seat, taking turns driving to Dublin—or, when their mother taught them about the Ottoman Empire, Constantinople. When a wheel gave way and the car lurched dangerously to one side, Francis told their parents not to let them play there.

The cushions that used to line the wide sill had been taken by the men and so Philip jumped up and stood in the recess. He had a better view of the valley than ever and he wondered why it had never occurred to him to try this before. Now he could see the mountains in the distance. The one with a summit like a boiled egg with the top lopped off was Mount Errigal, the highest mountain in Donegal, behind it was Muckish, or Dooish, he wasn't sure. He liked those names and wondered if they had been picked by children. If they had, what sort of adults had allowed such a privilege?

He jumped down from the sill and landed with a thud on the carpet. What would he do today? What was he *supposed* to do today? Surely there would be no lessons with his mother this morning, and he couldn't imagine what would happen in the afternoon. Usually, after he and Kate had lunch with Mrs. Connolly in the kitchen, they would go for a walk—if it was fine. Lately they'd been taking geography walks with their father, who would point out the features of the valley. Philip loved these afternoons. He saw much less of his father than his mother, despite the fact that his father's study wasn't far at all from the door to the upstairs drawing room where he and Kate did their morning lessons. When it rained, they would read books by the fire, curled up next to their mother. Kate was always the first to become restless, to walk to the window, to watch the water streaming down it, to suggest that they lived in the most boring place on earth. Their mother, Marianne, used to say, "Only boring people are bored," but lately she had given up and taken to ignoring Kate as best she could. Philip was glad of this. He didn't like feeling that it might have been better had they been born somewhere else—that there was a world sliding by without them.

It looked misty outside, but today there would be nowhere to read. Slumping onto the floor, his head banged against the bottom of the windowsill and then he banged it again, on purpose, for no good reason at all.

He sat there until his backside began to ache and he thought he'd better get up. He told himself that when he wanted to come back and look at Muckish and Dooish, he could. It was still his room. Dulough was still their house. Their father had told them so in his study after Christmas. He'd come to an arrangement with the government: Tourists would visit Dulough and the money they paid would fix the things that needed fixing, like the roof and the chimneys. It was very expensive to keep such a big house going and they didn't have the money to do it on their own anymore. Philip thought that Francis could have fixed things, but he didn't say it. The decision had been made.

On the landing it was surprisingly quiet. Philip had expected to see men everywhere, but aside from his feet creaking the same old floorboards that had creaked all his life, there was no sound. He wandered into the upstairs drawing room just in case he and Kate had been left some schoolwork to do. His mother would often leave them elaborate notes, assigning chapters to read, suggesting how long it might take them to do a certain lesson, how she would be back at a certain time (sharp!). But of course the drawing room was empty now, too. The long mahogany table where they did their work had left indentations in the carpet like the ones in his bedroom. The sofa with the sagging rose-patterned covers was gone, as was the sideboard that held all the board games and the old Meccano set. In the bay window, the wicker chair where his mother sat in the evenings had vanished too. The only thing left was the huge gilt-edged mirror, still hanging precariously above the fireplace. Philip looked up and saw himself reflected back, a scrawny boy in a green woolen jumper and blue corduroy trousers. He wondered if the mirror was being left behind for the tourists. With a bit of luck, he thought, it might squash one of them.

Above the main stairs, there was a long stain on the wall where the tapestry of the hunt had been. The hall was as dark as always, the only light coming in through the stained glass window at one end. Even on bright days, it was a gloomy, slightly frightening place, and on days like this, when the grayness seemed to have come down from the sky and settled on everything, he didn't like to be there at all. Ordinarily he took the servants' staircase, which began outside his bedroom door and went directly down into the kitchen. As the house didn't have servants anymore (except for Mrs. Connolly, who wasn't really a servant), he had never met anyone on the back stairs and considered them his territory.

Dulough's front door was big and heavy. It would have taken two Philips standing side by side with their arms stretched out to span its width. He stood on the ends of his toes, reached the latch, and put all his weight into pulling it towards him. Day filled the hall. The gravel swept in a semicircle around the front door; it was filled with chairs, tables, sideboards, beds (he could see his own), cupboards, bedside tables, armchairs, sofas, the wicker chair from the upstairs drawing room, and a rolled-up carpet. It was as if the house had taken a great breath and spat out its insides.

Each piece of furniture had a label that said either "Cottage" or "Dublin" in his mother's writing. He checked the labels on his things carefully; he was relieved to see that they all said "Cottage" on them.

24

Kate found him, sitting there on the rose-patterned couch, as she wove about the chaotic outdoor room. She was carrying an armful of plastic sheeting, which Philip recognized as the covering for the turf in the barn.

"We have to save all this before it's ruined. Mum said."

"Where is she?"

Kate was too busy pulling plastic over the dining room table to answer. He dragged a piece over to his bed. The sheets were still on it, just as he'd left them when the men took it away. He pulled them up.

"Come and help me with this, will you?" Kate shouted from the other side of the gravel, as she tried to cover the top of the very tall bookcases from the drawing room.

Philip made his way over to her.

"Why is all this stuff outside in the rain anyway?"

"Mum thinks the movers are useless," Kate answered, matter-of-factly. "They're over there, having lunch."

Philip looked down the avenue and saw a white van parked there. A thermos rested on the dashboard. They were not the men who'd come into his room.

"It's too early." He looked at his watch.

"They got here at seven, so it's their lunchtime now. They moved all the furniture when we were asleep."

Philip didn't like the idea that they had been dismantling the house as he slept upstairs. He thought that he shouldn't have been able to sleep through that, that he should have somehow known what was going on.

"What are we going to *do* today?" he asked Kate. "What are we supposed to be *doing*—I mean, if we haven't got schoolwork and stuff?"

"I think we're supposed to be helping."

"How?"

"I don't know, ask someone." She gestured to the bookcase.

He thought for a moment and said, "I'll help you, but then I'm going to look for the others."

When they had finished, the driveway looked like one of those slums in India that they'd seen in books, a plastic city with a life throbbing away underneath.

He rubbed the mist off his face with his sleeve and rounded the corner of the big house, passing between the pillars with the deer antlers on top. The avenue was rutted with puddles—he avoided them carefully because he wasn't wearing his boots. His father had told them that minibuses would carry the visitors from the main road up to the house. He tried to imagine what it would be like when Dulough was full of people, when there'd be lots of little buses on the avenue. He followed the curve of the lake for half a mile or so before the cottages came into view. The Connollys' was small and whitewashed, with a geranium-red half door and well-looked-after roses in the garden. Their own had appeared after Christmas—it magically grew out of the ground in the middle of the night, like a toadstool.

The only good part of this was that he'd be nearer to the Connollys—and the lake. Francis had taught him how to fish. Some days Philip would be summoned to their kitchen, with its frilly lace curtains and Virgin Marys lined up on the windowsill, for a decent meal. They were Francis's words. You had to have a decent meal before going fishing; with a decent bit of food in you, you could stay still out there for hours. He had heard his mother say that Francis reminded her of Yeats's fisherman. Philip found a book in the drawing room, *The Collected Works of W. B. Yeats*. He'd leafed through it until he came across the right poem. He agreed that a man with a "sun-freckled face" who went fishing at dawn was a good description of Francis, but he wasn't sure what the rest of the poem meant.

Because the new cottage floated on a sea of deep, sticky mud, a long, thin plank connected the avenue with the front door. It wobbled as Philip stepped onto it. He knew that if he fell in without his boots on, he'd certainly be in trouble. So as to make sure he didn't, he imagined that he was not surrounded with mud but with lava from a volcano. Mount Errigal had erupted after thousands of years, spewing its hot, liquid contents down the hillside. At any moment the new cottage and the Connollys' could melt. His survival depended on balancing on this fireproof bridge until he was rescued. He took a final leap and landed on the front porch.

Inside, his new home looked more like the outline of a house than a real one. There was no carpet on the floors and the doors had still to be hung. None of the furniture from the big house had arrived yet. He had come because he thought he might find his mother, but he knew the house was empty the moment he came in. Where was she? Usually, when she had to leave them, she'd say where she was going, which could only have been one of a few places—to the garden or to see Mrs. Connolly or to talk to their father in his study. But now it was as if she had vanished. He wanted to tell her about the men taking his bed before he was ready.

He wandered first into what was to be his parents' room. It was much smaller than their old one, whose great bay window looked out over the island, to the Atlantic. This room was dark;

damp advanced up the walls. Though it was morning and the window was curtainless, it let in little light. Philip mentally positioned the bed, their wardrobe and chest of drawers, his father's chair. He wondered how they'd all fit. Next he went into his new room. It was the twin of Kate's; both rooms looked out over the lake at the back, the lake from which the house took its name: Dulough meant "black lake" in Irish. Francis had told Philip this because Philip hadn't started learning Irish yet. It would be good to see the water each morning and to imagine all the fish teeming just below the surface, waiting to be caught. Perhaps they'd let him moor the boat there. He should have asked about that.

Outside, there was still no movement from the men in the white van. They were sleeping off their lunch. On the gravel, the wind blew up the corners of the plastic city and allowed the rain to soak Philip's bed, so that he wouldn't be able to sleep on it. He would be with Kate in her new room and they would fight over the covers.

That night, for the first time in its life, the big house was empty. The wind still flew down the valley and rattled Philip's windows, but their owner was not there to imagine them blowing in. The deer herd came down as close as they dared to the house and sheltered amongst the Scots pines. Below them, at the end of the garden, where cliffs gave way to the Atlantic, it was sea, sea, all the way to America.

John

If he is going to leave, he needs to leave now, before the men come, before dawn. He rises in the half-light, his trousers on the chair where he left them. No clean shirt; that would mean opening the wardrobe and waking Marianne. His wife is still asleep, head sunk deeply into the pillow. She wears a nightgown that she made herself, lace up to the neck and buttons down the front; it reaches all the way to her toes and is warmer, she tells him, than any of the ones they make nowadays, the ones you'd get from Dunnes or Penneys. As he laces his shoes, without socks, because they, too, are in the wardrobe, he watches his sleeping wife.

Outside, he walks away from the house. The dawn comes up over the lake, sliding down the hills and across the water. He is tired and, for the lack of a shirt, already cold, his woolen jumper itching his bare skin. Save for when he was at school and college, he has never lived anywhere but here. His parents sent him away at seven. It was what their sort of people did then, but he resolved in those first weeks, his classmates sleeping around him, that once he was old enough, he would return to Dulough for good.

It hadn't surprised him that Marianne was happy to leave the place where she'd grown up; though he'd got used to Dublin when he was in college, he knew that it was impossible to be as attached to the city as to the country. She took to Dulough easily, running the gardens, designing a new one where there was a natural rise and plateau behind the house, before the hills proper. It is an Oriental garden, perfectly square, with four small temples on long columns at each corner, and flowers that grow so symmetrically they seem unreal. A statue of the Buddha sits in the middle, smiling benignly at the horizon. None of his own family would have thought of that. The statue was ordered from India, from a village called Bodh Gaya, where they say the Buddha found enlightenment. It arrived unbroken, but now the daily rain weathers it at a ferocious pace.

Marianne spends afternoons on the grounds, usually alone, but sometimes with Francis or the children. John is much more nervous about her reaction to strangers roaming there than the house. The government has given her a field of rocky soil on the headland, and she has taken cuttings from her favorite plants, moving them up, out of the way of the tourists. She has planted a barrier of rhododendrons, which he knows she is counting on to knit together and shield her garden from the world.

John has been so immersed in arrangements for the move, in meetings with the government men, with Frank Foyle, with Mr. Murphy, that he had not considered the possibility that he would wake up this morning and go—that he would not be in the thick of it all. He hasn't had time to imagine what the house might look like emptied of all its contents, as blank spaces and marked walls. And because he can imagine it now, he leaves. The house's insides haven't changed from the day the walls were originally papered, the furniture positioned in configurations conceived of by the first Philip, who had come to Ireland from Scotland in the years after the Famine. If anything would disturb his ancestor's ghost, allowing strangers to walk the house would surely be it. What John has more difficulty with is what his parents and grandparents would think; they managed to keep the estate going through the various wars. They survived, a world unto themselves. His mother told him that as a child, it had been her job to cut up old newspapers and stack them neatly next to the loo. Marianne wouldn't think much of that. In college, it irked him when she had chosen expensive places to eat—restaurants that cost half the price would have done just as well. But he soon understood that she liked a sense of occasion.

He often wondered whether she felt that she had been lured to Dulough under false pretenses. Though he hadn't deliberately lied about his finances, he hadn't been forthcoming when he asked her to marry him. He would not admit it to Marianne, but he is, in many ways, relieved by the deal. The estate is an expensive place to run. His mother, in a fit of benevolent stupidity, willed him the house and his brother most of the money that was left to run it. John thought that he and Marianne would be able to live on the few investments he did have, and from renting out the fields. But he had calculated badly; it hadn't been enough for a long time now.

Marianne would have been forgiven for thinking that she would have stability and peace. This had certainly been true for her in the first ten years of their life together. John was quite proud that he had managed to hide the fact that they were running out of money fast. Mrs. Connolly knew, though; she took in the post in the mornings and deduced that the "Final Reminder" stamped across the tops of bills was not simply John's absent-mindedness. She encouraged him to confide in Marianne. There shouldn't be secrets between husbands and wives, she said. Mrs. Connolly hadn't asked then about her own future at Dulough, or Francis's—whether she could not conceive that they would ever do without her, or from a desire not to add to John's worries, he couldn't tell. He had been remiss not to reassure her then, he thinks.

It took him the best part of a year to tell Marianne. It was two summers ago now. They had all spent the day on the beach, the children running up and down from the water to where an orange three-man tent had been pitched beyond the tide line, to shield them from the wind and the sudden rain showers. They picnicked in there at lunchtime, Kate and Philip wrapped in towels, their hair slicked back against their smooth skulls, their legs, plastered in sand, tucked underneath them. Philip brought a crab into the tent and it scuttled about the sides, desperately looking for a way to get out. John picked it up by its shell and took Philip down to the water so that they could watch it return to the sea. "He'll like it better there, don't you think?" But he could see that Philip wasn't so sure. He watched as his son wrestled with whether to cry. From Marianne, he had learnt to turn away from the children at moments like this. To them, it was only worth crying when they had an audience. He walked back up the beach to where she was cleaning up the picnic.

As John had watched her buttering bread for the children, so fully ensconced in Dulough, so much a part of the place, he realized that he would be able to tell her then without any possibility of her reneging on their agreement—which was their marriage—and returning to the city. Before the children, he'd wondered if she might have left if things hadn't gone smoothly; he had worried that he wasn't enough of an anchor for her. The worry persisted, even now, perhaps more than ever now, as they left the big house for the cottage. But he might have been selling her short to have believed she could go.

That night, after they'd come up from the beach and bathed the children, fed them supper and put them to bed, their noses red from an unusual amount of sun, he told her. She had been stoical, more concerned with his feelings than her own, determined to look on the bright side. After all, the tourists would only be there for half the year; the rest of the time they would continue in glorious isolation. The last bit she said with a wry smile, which he hadn't been quite sure how to interpret.

But John had tried to make money, hadn't he? The trouble was that Donegal was not an easy place to find a job. He supposed that he could have taken a flat in Dublin during the week and come up and down at the weekend. But who would have schooled the children? Marianne couldn't have done it on her own. And she wouldn't have liked being the only one in the house at night, Kate and Philip waking in the small hours, hungry or thirsty, or in need of a cuddle after a bad dream. She was childlike herself sometimes.

There had been the various schemes to try to make the estate pay for itself. But, over the years, he had been forced to sell off one piece of property and then another, remnants of his family's holdings, in Scotland and abroad, in Africa, and in countries he barely recognized the names of. These investments amazed him—that a firm somewhere in London had been buying and selling on their behalf for the best part of a hundred and fifty years. Of course, he'd had to have Phil's signature for these sales too. His brother had been surprisingly willing to sell the last of the family's investments, out of guilt, John supposed, that he had nothing to do with the estate anymore. Phil phoned him when they sold the last investment. They talked then about what should be done, and it was Phil who'd come up with the idea that Dulough might be a tourist attraction. People visited stately homes all the time, and if Dulough wasn't quite stately, Phil was certain that could be made up for by its eccentric design, by the unusual gardens and beautiful scenery. John was surprised at Phil's description; he had never heard his brother talk about the estate in such positive terms.

He needs to stop lingering in the garden; he wants to get away from the house before he is seen out a window and called back to what really is his duty. He knows that he is not doing the honorable thing by disappearing on this day of all days. Moving through the kitchen garden, following a path overgrown with purple foxgloves and rhododendrons, he is in the foothills of the valley. The grass is wet and knee-high; the water soaks through his trousers. The valley is so steep that he cannot climb straight up. He zigzags in wide arcs to reach the top. Thin ribbons of pathways, worn by the deer, mark the way. Their tracks are beginning to grow over and there is no dung; they haven't been by in a while. He doesn't much like the deer; they are impressive from far away, especially the males, with their huge antlers, but up close they are like any large animal, unclean and unpredictable. They are one of the last herds of red deer in Ireland, and even if the tourists aren't likely to ever see them, it gives Dulough the air of a wildlife preserve, which he hopes will be another attraction when the gates open.

Turning to see how high he has climbed, he looks down. The roof is a dark, uneven shape below him, with turrets and crenulated walls sprouting off in all directions, the gardens a patchwork quilt of greens. But it is not the gardens he loves. The mountains are covered in rock—scree, boulders. Near the ridge, the grass has been shorn away by the wind to reveal patches of granite underneath, like raw flesh under skin. The water that fills the bottom of the valley is colder than the sea. When the children were small, he and Marianne would row them from the moorings behind the house to the other side of the lake for picnics. Philip took a liking to the little boat, and sometimes they rowed about the lake, just the two of them. When he hadn't the time, Francis was kind about doing it. Kate was Francis's favorite, though. When she was little, she followed him around the gardens as he worked, and when she wanted to follow him into the hills, he made an Eskimo-style sling so that he could carry her on his back, her little legs dangling above his own. When John didn't approve, Marianne asked him if he thought it was dangerous, but wasn't no one safer up there than Francis?

As he'd explained to Francis that the estate was to be opened to the public, the old man showed no concern, as John had expected, for the house or for the gardens, only for Kate and

Philip. But Francis wasn't the one who watched the bank accounts, and Francis wasn't responsible for the bills—any of them—not even the electricity in his and his wife's cottage. John took care of that, too.

When Marianne was pregnant with Kate, John had resolved that their children would stay with them in Donegal—that they would be schooled at home until they went to the local secondary school. But it might not be a bad idea for the children to go away after all, to shield them from all this upheaval. Each time he considered Francis's reaction to the news, he got more worried about the effect the move was having on Kate and Philip. How would they react to the loss of their home, to the sudden presence of strangers?

His eyes follow the contours of the hills, up to Errigal and down again to Dooish. The landscape is so familiar that he knows it better than his own body, better than his children's bodies.

Philip is very thin and very white; the doctor told them to make sure he had a decent glass of milk every day so as to fatten him up. Years of decent glasses of milk have not fattened Philip up, but it doesn't seem to have done him any harm; he is perfectly capable of fending for himself, more so than his sister, who looks much healthier. Kate and Philip are infinitely better nourished than John was as a child; his memories are full of white bread and cakes and orange squash, whereas Marianne won't let Mrs. Connolly feed the children anything but vegetables and organic meat.

A man is walking towards John across the top of the ridge. He wears a ragged shirt and tie under an old tweed jacket, as if he left the house in his Sunday best and dragged himself through a thicket. It is Owen Mór, who owns the land adjacent to Dulough.

The old farmer is trespassing, and John wonders how often he passes from his own land onto theirs. He is watching the bottom of the valley. When John looks in the same direction, he sees the moving lorry winding its way up the avenue towards the house. It's followed by a small white van. He glances at his watch; they're late. Still, it has given him time to get well out of the way. When he looks up again, Owen Mór is staring directly at him. His face hasn't changed from when he thought he was alone; his mouth is a thin, lipless line almost hidden by a white half-grown beard. Some sort of sheepdog-collie mix limps up behind him, as expressionless as his owner.

"Having some work done?" Owen Mór says, as soon as the men are close enough to hear each other above the wind. He does not seem at all embarrassed being caught on someone else's land. John looks down at the house, but the lorry and the van have disappeared into the trees at the end of the avenue. It is easiest to say yes, but as soon as he does, Owen Mór's lips bend into a half smile. He should have remembered that the old farmer is thick with Frank Foyle, the local county councillor in charge of turning Dulough into a tourist attraction. Owen Mór seems to recognize this knowledge in John and tries again. "That'll be the movers, then?"

"Yes, I think so."

If Owen Mór is wondering what John is doing all the way up here, he doesn't mention it. "Nice morning, so it is."

He turns away and walks on across the top of the ridge in the direction of the sea. John watches him disappear over the hill. He climbs the few more steps it takes to get to the top, the knife-edge of the ridge, which the older man had taken like a mountain goat a few moments before. John hasn't been up here in years, since before the children were born, perhaps, and he is surprised to discover that he is more afraid than he was as a younger man—that the possibility of falling now seems quite real.

He sees the land around him as if he were on a plane. The world outside Dulough is a series of messy fields, Lough Power a vast green pool in the distance. Green, not black; it is much shallower than John's own lake. The English artist Edward Steele lives at Lough Power now, finally having claimed his great-grandfather's house after it had been left uninhabited for so long. Unlike his ancestor Geoffrey Roe, who was a painter, Steele works in wood and metal. He has placed sculptures in the shallow waters of the lough, a hollow dolphin and a larger-than-life salmon. John has always meant to ask if he could bring Kate and Philip to see the iron fish in the water.

It is still early in the morning and he knows that the movers are likely to be around all day. He is cold; he has had nothing to eat. But he's well used to walking, and his legs keep moving whether he wills them to or not. He follows the top of the ridge north, away from the sea, naming the geographical features as he walks; he is trying not to think about the blister forming on his right heel. He should have worn yesterday's socks; they would have been better than nothing.

When he reaches the cirque at the end of the valley, he scrambles down to the bottom and pulls off his shoe; one heel is soaked with blood. He lowers his foot into a tea-colored pool, the top layer warmed by the sun, and lies back on the rock, keeping his foot in the water, making a comfortable bed on the moss with his jacket. The house, the cottages, the moving men, even Owen Mór, disappear from view; he is completely encased in mountain. He remembers hiding up here late one summer, on a morning when he was due to return to boarding school, when the thought of the place made him sick. It had taken them hours to find him: his mother and father and Francis's predecessor, a man named Thom O'Connor, all traipsing around the gardens and up into the hills, before finally tracking him down here, at the lip of the tarn, cold, but not much wet, and happy. He knew that by the time they got him ready to go, he'd miss at least the first day, which he did. As did his brother, who, always more intrepid than John, didn't hide his scorn that his younger sibling resorted to such tricks. The similarity between that day and this isn't lost on him now.

Hours later he walks on towards home, trying to calculate the movers' progress. They might have left the house and gone down to the cottage—or they might have finished altogether. He can't see Marianne and the children like this, disheveled and a little bloody. When he opens the gate to the gardens, the moving men have indeed disappeared. Crunching across the gravel, he tries to open Dulough's front door. It's locked. It takes him a few moments to absorb that he must go around to the back.

The kitchen looks as it always has, saucepans hanging from hooks above the range, the row of porcelain hot water bottles on a shelf by the door, the battery of servants' bells labeled "Drawing Room," "Dining Room," "Bedroom One," "Bedroom Two," all the way up to "Ten." Grateful that the kitchen hasn't changed, he moves through the passage into the house proper. The hall has always been a bare room, if one can call a hall a room, but now it is utterly empty. Even the tapestry of the hunt has been taken, leaving a long, dark stain on the wall. The drawing room and dining room are empty too, but for their gold mirrors, still hanging over the fireplaces, too big to go anywhere but there. They reflect the rooms back twice their size and so, like the hall, they seem much bigger than before. Now that the furniture is gone, he can see the colors the wallpaper used to be, a deep burgundy in the dining room, and in the drawing room, a silvery moss green.

He has almost grown used to the empty spaces but when he finally goes upstairs, his own bedroom shocks him. Where he left his sleeping wife that morning, there is a spool of twine on the carpet. In that strange duality that can exist in the mind, the one that allows us to make two appointments at three o'clock on the same day, John, knowing that the furniture would be gone, has come up here to get a clean shirt and a pair of socks from his wardrobe. He looks out the bay window, glad that the view is the same as always when what is behind him has changed so completely. Because the bed was the last place he saw Marianne, he half believes that she has disappeared and he feels the need to find her, to see if she is all right.

He goes into the bathroom adjoining their bedroom; if he is honest, he looks better than expected. The walk has done him good. His cheeks are pink, like his daughter's, and he looks somewhat rested. But that doesn't solve the problem of not having a shirt; without it, he looks strange, not himself at all. When he puts his nose in his jumper to see whether it smells very bad, he realizes that a V-shape has been tattooed into his chest by the sun and the wind. He splashes water on his face and puts some in his hair, running his fingers through it as best he can; there is no comb and no towel. Really, he needs a bath. The bottom of his right trouser leg still has some blood on it, but he hopes not noticeably so. Fortunately, downstairs, no one has thought to remove the old coats that hang above a line of boots by the back door. He rummages in the coats and comes up with a scarf, which he ties neatly around his neck as he makes his way down the avenue to his new home.

In the cottage, he finds Marianne in Philip's room, pulling the wet bedclothes off his bed.

"Darling." Marianne brushes her hair out of her eyes. "Where have you *been?*"

He quiets her by putting his hands over her ears and kissing her on the forehead, relieved to have found her.

"In town. What can I do to help?"

Philip

The morning after the move, Philip and Kate escaped the new cottage to go swimming. Built years ago in Dulough's ramparts, the pool was separated from the lake by a low, lichen-encrusted wall, so that from far away it was impossible to tell where the pool stopped and the lake began.

In the cottage, they had slipped their swimming togs on under their clothes. They knew that there was nothing for it but to throw them off and dive in without thinking. To pause was to be beaten by the icy water, and neither was going to give up in front of the other. Each year, when the weather got warmer, in May or June, Francis would drain the pool of its winter casualties. There were the usual leaves, rotted, disintegrated, but there were other things too, things which had sunk to the bottom—birds, mice, even badgers. When the water froze, Philip and Kate could see the carcasses suspended there, halfway between the surface and the bottom of the pool. When it unfroze, Francis scooped them out with a net, their animal skin falling away from their bones. This ritual had not yet been performed; the children would have to try not to think about what was below them.

Philip was first in. Kate hesitated for a moment, watching as the debris closed over the hole he made in the water. A few seconds went by. She ran at the pool and jumped high into the air, careful to miss where his body might be. When she came up, there he was, laughing, spluttering. "Ha, ha," he said gleefully. She pushed his head under, only now registering the cold shock of the water that had not so long ago been ice.

After Francis fished out the pool's winter catch, he would drain it and give the blue bottom a good scrubbing. The children would help him throw the buckets of hot, soapy water, which he spread around with a coarse-bristled sweeping brush. The paint was chipped now, and the blue was marred by clouds of white. Francis said that it could do with being repainted, but there wasn't the money, and there were more important things to be fixed. As they swam in circles, Philip stopped and asked Kate whether it would be painted now that the tourists were coming.

"Prob-ly not," she said. "I don't think people from warm places would want to swim in a cold Irish pool."

When Francis had finished, it was refilled with clean water, but it was mostly rain they were swimming in now. He would kill them if he knew. But the gasping, freezing shock of jumping in had done them both good. It erased, if only for a few moments, the dullness that had settled on them since yesterday.

They were grateful that there was enough hot water when they got back to the cottage for them to have baths. When they sat back down at the kitchen table, their skin still tingled. Kate put the tea on; as they drank, they made shapes from the damp that had risen up to stain the bare concrete floor. Philip saw a tree and a car, Kate traced the outline of a jagged mountain with her finger. The walls were bare, too. According to their mother, most of Dulough's pictures were far too big to fit into such a cramped little house. But the furniture had slid magically into the places Philip had thought it would go. The mahogany wardrobe towered over his parents' room and seemed to lean in slightly, as if, were the earth to tremor, it would fall flat on the bed. The bed itself had been pushed into a space under the window; the iron headboard with its gold swirls reached nearly all the way to the ceiling. There was room for only one bedside table, and Philip wondered which of his parents would get it. It reminded him of the dwellings from *The Wind in the Willows,* the tiny rooms eked out of the riverbank or the trunk of a tree, with furniture cluttered about, far too much of it, so that Mole and Ratty could barely move.

When they had finished their tea, they began their work. At Philip's insistence, their father had set them some geography at nine. It was nearly eleven now and they'd have to hurry to get it done before lunch. Kate began drawing in a listless, halfhearted way. Philip got up and went to the window.

"What are you doing?" she asked.

"Looking at the valley."

"Why?"

"Because I want to draw it."

Kate sighed in exasperation. She was annoyed that Philip had reminded their father to set them schoolwork.

"There's one in *this* book, that you can *trace;* it'll be a lot easier."

"But I want to draw *our* valley, not that one."

"We don't have time—here."

She thrust their textbook in his direction and pointed at the perfectly symmetrical glaciated valley. He took the book from her, glanced at the picture, and then let his eyes wander back to his favorite passage:

During the last ice age, glaciers covered much of Ireland. When they finally melted, a new country had been fashioned out of the old landscape. Snow collected on the mountains and turned to ice, which pushed down into the rock in a circular motion, forming what geographers call a **corrie** *or* **cirque** *(from the French word for circus, because the geographical feature they formed resembled an upside-down big top). Soon the ice would find a weakness in the side of the cirque and spill over the lip. It made its way down the mountainside, gathering momentum, pulling branches, rocks, soil and other debris with it (the correct term is* **moraine***) until it became a great river of ice, gouging its way to the sea. The glacier followed the path of the river that went before it, obliterating the old terrain and forming a* **U-shaped valley,** *which, over the years, would fill with water and become a deep lake with steep sides....*

Philip had read and reread this section. He was fascinated to think that thousands of years ago Dulough looked quite different than it did now, that there had been no lake but a river, winding its way down to the sea. And ice so deep that it swallowed up everything in its path. If the house and cottages had been around then, it would have swept them away, too. Before reading about glaciation, he had never considered that his world had not always been just as he saw it, and he felt suddenly more grown-up to be armed with this information.

Kate had nearly finished drawing the textbook U-shaped valley into her notebook. Theirs was not nearly so neat and tidy. Philip got up again and looked out the window above the sink. The valley in the book was a theoretical one, and in that, it was perfect, with evenly spaced cirques and hanging valleys, as well as symmetrical-looking scree. He was determined to draw Dulough just as it was now, but he would leave out anything he wasn't sure how to label.

Kate said, "If you don't hurry up and get that done, they're going to know we weren't here all morning."

Their mother was the first to return home. She burst through the back door with such force that the door hit the wall behind and shuddered. She made sure that the glass hadn't broken and turned to encounter her children sitting at the kitchen table, looking up at her in surprise. She was not usually one for door banging, and Philip wondered whether she had almost forgotten that she had two children, doing their lessons in the new kitchen, in the little house with the damp walls. Now she stood by the sink, watching them and swaying slightly.

"Look at my drawing." He held it up for her. "It's Dulough."

Kate looked at him as if he were an idiot. She took her mother's hand loosely.

"What's wrong?" she asked.

Philip's picture was forgotten. He shouldn't have shown it to her until it was completely finished. He wanted her to say that it was very good.

"The gardeners took a huge chunk out of the lawn to widen the path. Apparently there wouldn't have been enough room for the visitors to walk otherwise."

There was a new accent on the way his mother said "visitors." Before, she had tried to make it sound smooth, almost welcoming, but the word had hard edges now. This inflection bothered Philip more than her distress. Leaving his mum and Kate in the kitchen, he slipped quietly out the front door. When he got to the big house, a different van to that of the movers was parked outside; it was dark green and said T. BOYLE & SONS, LAND- SCAPERS on each side. The last word had vines curling around it, as if they'd sprouted from the letters. There was a white car, too: OFFICE OF PUBLIC WORKS, it said. They were the people in charge of Dulough now. They were the government, or part of the government, Philip wasn't sure, but his father insisted that the family should be proud that Dulough was being made accessible to the Irish people. There was no one in either of the cars, but the front door of the house stood open, as if someone had just been through.

Philip crouched behind a rhododendron, not far from the top of the cliffs, where two rows of trees marked the end of the demesne and the beginning of the sea. There was a steep drop of at least fifty feet behind him; there the garden ended and the beach began. He looked out over the lawn; one side had been churned up from green grass to black earth. A piece of orange twine ran the length of it, marking where the new path would be. It was three or four times as wide as the old one. At the end nearest him, two men were digging up the last part of it. They hadn't noticed Philip and worked in silence, stopping only to slide packets of cigarettes out of their pockets. They smoked three each in half an hour, holding them between their yellowed thumbs and forefingers and sucking on them like straws as their boots sank into the mud.

When the men had finished, they moved off in the direction of the higher gardens. Philip came out of his hiding place. They had turned up roots, worms, rocks, and a stream that ran under the old path towards the sea. Their work had disturbed its course and the water had begun to pool, swirling with earth, in the newly turned ground. Philip knew that if it wasn't fixed, the whole lawn would be a pond by morning. That would upset his mother even more.

First he picked out the bigger rocks; he would use them to make a channel for the water. He laid them carefully on the old path so that they wouldn't sink back into the mud. Before he began his work, he picked up one of the longer cigarette ends and stuck it in his mouth; it was wet, but he moved it to the corner of his lips, like the men had, and it warmed up. When he had fixed the stream, he watched as it flowed, trickling over humps in the earth and brimming with butts and earthworms, away to the head of the cliffs.

He was very dirty. The water had seeped over the tops of his boots, he had patches of mud on his knees, his hands were black. On his way back to the cottage, he noticed that the gardeners' van had disappeared, leaving tire marks in the gravel, but the white car was still there. He crouched under the drawing room window. Three people sat, two men and a lady, on camp chairs around the unlit fireplace. They each had a teacup and there was a plate of biscuits on the floor in front of them. The lady was writing in a notebook. The younger man was gesturing, cutting the air in half with sweeps of his hands.

Mrs. Connolly came in with a teapot, the one she used for good, and refilled their cups. Philip shrank back into the bushes. Without looking at her, the man put his hand over the top of his cup when she went to fill it. A drop of tea fell from the spout onto his white, freckled skin. He carried on talking as if nothing had happened, and Mrs. Connolly was away out the door, back to the kitchen.

Philip took one more look at the people from the government and went inside the big house. He hoped there weren't any more of them lurking about the place, that they were all safely penned up in the drawing room. The patterns of his old home had changed. Before, he was able to say to himself, "Mummy is in the drawing room, Daddy is in his study, Kate is in the kitchen with Mrs. Connolly…" They had revolved around each other like planets on preset courses. But now there might be a chance encounter with a stranger as he went up to his room, a stranger who would tell him that he shouldn't be there.

He ran up the stairs as fast as he could, glad of his stocking feet, and into his bedroom. It was the first time he'd come back since the move and it was exactly how he'd left it, except that it was colder than before. He went over to the window and jumped up onto the ledge, his socks slipping on the slick paint. Muckish and Dooish were there, their summits covered in white cloud that spilled over the top and down the sides, like cream on a Christmas pudding.

Philip got back to the cottage in the late afternoon, when the hills were beginning to get dark. He had missed lunch and it was not yet time for supper. A cold roast beef sandwich sat on the kitchen table with a note beside it from his mother. It seemed relatively cheerful: *Gone for a walk. Back later. Mummy, x x x.* He sat down at the table and lifted up the corners of the brown bread. He did not like roast beef, and he especially did not like cold roast beef, the way it hardened and you had to tear at it with your teeth if you wanted to bite some off. He got up and went to the fridge to see if there was anything else to eat, but there was only milk and butter, and a plate with more cold meat on it.

As he sat back down at the table, his father came in. Taking off his coat, he hung it on the hook behind the back door and smoothed down his hair. His father was always more smartly dressed than his mother. He wore ties every day, even to go on their walks. When they'd gone a particularly long way or climbed a very steep hill, he would stop, undo the top button of his shirt, and loosen the knot of his tie, turning to survey how far they'd come.

"Oh, hello there," he said. Like Philip's mother, he too looked surprised to see his son in their new little house.

"I don't like roast beef sandwiches," Philip said, "but there isn't anything else."

"Really?" His father smiled.

"Yes." Philip paused for a moment, and then, as a wave of disgust rose in him at the stringy meat, he added, "Mummy was upset today because the men from the government ruined the garden."

"Where's Mummy now?" His father's face twisted, for a moment, into a look Philip hadn't seen before.

"Gone for a walk." Philip handed him the note. And before he could show him his drawing of the valley or tell him about damming the stream, his father went back through the door without even bothering to take his coat.

John

As the children swam in the icy pool, John was on his way to an appointment with the county councillor. When he arrived in town, the bells were tolling for mass. The Catholic church towered over the main street, an ugly building with hulking flying buttresses, too many statues, and an overcrowded graveyard. John liked Father Damien, though, a priest who was not afraid to creep up behind his parishioners in the newsagent's and ask why they hadn't been to confession lately. It was because John didn't come under Father Damien's jurisdiction that they got on so well.

He parked the car on the bridge over the river that cut the town in two. Malachy's pub was the closest building to the water and it did well in seafood and Guinness when the tourists came. It must seem terribly authentic to them, John thought, an old whitewashed Donegal farmhouse, with family photographs on the windowsills, watching as you ate. It made him wonder what the tourists would make of Dulough. It would be quite a different experience altogether.

The town was quiet. A few people scurried between the butcher's, the hardware shop, and the Spar, clutching bags. They paid John no attention and he was glad of this as he walked up the road. Frank Foyle's office was above Driver's, a shop that sold goods like walking boots and fishing rods. John rang the bell and waited. He shivered in his shirtsleeves; it was not as warm as it had been the day before. Frank Foyle's secretary came downstairs; her name was Nancy. She was a buxom, cowlike girl. She'd only left school a year or two ago, but she looked much, much older. Her face was covered in a deep, heavy layer of makeup. Smiling broadly, she said, "How are you, Mr. Campbell?" with the implication that there was no need for an answer.

"Hello there, Nancy." He'd come to know her quite well over the past year or so, having waited often in the outer office where her desk was while Frank Foyle readied himself for these visits. He felt sorry for Nancy. There were few prospects in the area for girls like her; the ones with any ambition went to Dublin or London. The best John could do was plant the idea in her mind that perhaps Councillor Foyle wasn't the best choice of employer, that she might be better off somewhere else. Of course, this was a delicate thing to suggest, but he feared that he'd been too subtle. He had often wondered whether she had a boyfriend, a local she might eventually marry, someone who'd build her a nice house and protect her from the Foyles of the world. She would make a good mother, he thought; she was kind, she had sympathy for him and Marianne, he could tell by her manner. He wondered whether there might be a place for her at Dulough now; perhaps she could be trained as a guide or employed in the office overseeing the construction of the Visitors' Center. He must ask Murphy.

Foyle arrived at his office door, hand outstretched, boots caked in mud and, by the smell of it, dung. "Good to see you, sir," he said.

A mahogany desk, resembling a coffin, dominated the small room. The county councillor plunged back into his ergonomic chair; there was no such luxury for his guests. What John perched on was hard, wooden, decidedly school-like. Councillor Foyle made John uneasy. He wasn't sure how much irony was in the "sir." He knew that Mr. Foyle relished this deal and his own part in it, that he felt things were being righted; Irish land was being returned to the Irish people. Besides, the town needed the jobs that the estate would provide. John had to stifle the urge to remind Foyle that the house still belonged to him, that the government was only looking after the upkeep for the time being. The panic that had caused him to flee the moving men yesterday morning returned.

"That'll be two cups of tea, Nancy, thanks," Foyle said, as he got up again to shut the door with his boot.

He looked closely at John in a manner he wouldn't have had the guts for a year earlier.

"I spoke to your wife yesterday. She said the move was going smoothly."

So Marianne knew he hadn't been in town. He should have thought of a better excuse. But he'd no time to dwell on it; a piece of paper was being pushed towards him across the cluttered desk. The thought of visitors arriving in four weeks' time was suddenly too much.

"Mr. Foyle, I'm still of the same mind about the opening date. The estate won't be ready in a month."

What difference would it make if they opened the gates a little later? The weather would be better in June anyway.

Frank Foyle's mouth puckered. John knew him well enough by now to realize that the politician was annoyed, that he was trying to choose his words carefully.

"We've printed the publicity materials with the May opening date already, Mr. Campbell. Paddy Friel's putting them up this morning. And didn't you say yourself that the house was in need of a new chimney?"

"It is," John paused. "That's precisely what I'm saying, we should wait until the repairs are finished."

"Ah, but rebuilding the chimney is a big investment that will require a lot of capital. Michael—Mr. Murphy—and me have decided that we need to see how the business does before we invest heavily in the venture."

John should have known that he couldn't trust Foyle. He thought miserably about the crumbling chimney, about the rotten window frames, about the missing roof tiles.

"That wasn't our agreement," he said weakly.

"We didn't have an agreement about the chimney, sir. We don't have agreements about any *specific* improvements. If you'd like to peruse the documents again, you will see that the Office of Public Works hasn't said what it will and will not repair. We have no particular obligations in that sense. What we do have is an agreement to build the Visitors' Center, tarmacadam the roadway up to the house, provide you with three minibuses and drivers, staff for the kitchen, a guide for the tours, and a salary for yourself and Mr. Francis Connolly and Mrs. Mary Connolly until yous all reach retirement age. After that, sir, your son—or daughter—remains the owner, of course, but we've no salary obligations towards them."

Frank Foyle pushed the final contracts a little further in John's direction and sat back in his chair. John signed without reading. Mr. Foyle's tongue poked out the corner of his mouth, following the direction of John's signature across the page. When John handed the papers back, Foyle made a show of bundling them together and putting them inside a leather case.

John had never thought of his family as privileged. They had lived in a grand house, yes, but they'd had no luxuries. And yet he realized now that he *had* been spoilt. He had been brought up to think that there would always be enough money, magically there, because people like them always had enough. It was unthinkable that they would have to compromise themselves to accept a job they didn't want, a job that might take them away from Dulough, a patch of Ireland they had a right to.

"Nancy!" Frank Foyle bellowed, as he put the case in the top drawer of his desk and locked it with a key that seemed much too small for his farmer's fingers to grasp.

She came to the door.

"Yes?"

"Change those teas to whiskeys."

"The tea's made."

"Tea would be fine." John turned to Nancy and smiled.

Foyle ignored him and gave her a look somewhere between brazen lust and fatherly scolding. John didn't turn to see what sort of expression Nancy might conjure up in return, but the door shut and he heard the clink of glasses in the outer office.

The councillor's seat snapped forwards when Nancy entered with a bottle.

"To your health, sir," he said. "It's been a pleasure doing business with you and your good wife."

John took a drink of the whiskey, trying to hide the loathing he felt for this man.

Nancy had returned to her desk; her computer keyboard clacked loudly beyond the door. John wished he'd brought one of the children with him so that he could excuse himself sooner. Yesterday, he had been sure that Marianne would understand why he had to leave, that she would forgive him, especially as he'd blamed his absence on a meeting with Foyle. But when they got into bed, she'd turned her face to the wall and drawn her knees up to her chin. He should have known that there was more to her silence than simply irritation that he'd disappeared when the movers arrived.

What glee this man must have found in catching him in a falsehood, in covering for him in his self-righteous manner: "Don't worry, Marianne; I'm sure he's his reasons." And how much it would have annoyed her to have learnt that John hadn't been in town after all, from this little man, whom she deplored. It was no wonder that her anger had carried over into this morning, that she hadn't made him breakfast, that she'd ignored him as he wandered, lost, around the new, bare kitchen, looking for a tea bag and a slice of bread.

John finished his whiskey and put the glass down on Foyle's desk. He realized that the county councillor had been studying him as he drank, and he had the horrible feeling that the man could tell what he was thinking. He had felt more comfortable in the larger meetings, more of a businessman drawing up a deal

than someone in need of financial assistance from the government. He and Foyle were partners, two Donegal men, fighting
for the good of a local treasure, against the city bureaucrats. But
that feeling was gone now. The passage of this year had broken
him down. He remembered his early dealings with Frank Foyle.
John was the man from the big house, from a family who had remained prosperous for centuries, a family who had given work
to local men in the post-Famine years. But John needed the government now, more than they needed him, and he had seen the
click of recognition when they realized. With that, he had felt as
if he were evaporating, as if he was somehow diminished with
each meeting, so that now he was weak and had been weakened
for good.

Outside the office, he stopped to collect himself.

A voice behind him said, "Mr. Campbell, how are you keeping?"

It was Mrs. Baskin, the chemist. She was always very well
turned out, even when she served in the shop. Marianne had
drawn his attention to this one day, after filling a prescription for
Kate. She mused that Mrs. Baskin could have done better. "Better than what?" John had wondered. Marianne was still relatively
new to Dulough then and he hadn't dared to ask whether she
meant "better than here."

"So you'll be opening those gates to the tourists then?"

Surely the posters couldn't be up already, John thought.

"It was only that Mary was in the other day," she added.

So it had been Mrs. Connolly. There was no point in getting
het up about it, the news would be out soon anyway.

"I might come up and have a look at the place myself—if I
can get someone to mind the shop. I mean if it's all right with
you, but if the tourists..."

Her voice trailed off. John saw that it was his job now to be polite. "Yes, yes. Of course. Please do. You'd be very welcome." He'd better get used to this.

Twenty minutes later, as he swung the car into the muddy driveway outside the new cottage, he was surprised that instinct had not made him drive up to the big house. Through the window, he could see his son sitting at the table. Philip looked around expectantly when he heard the door open and watched in silence as his father took off his coat and hung it on the hook behind the door. John was taken aback by Philip's appearance; he seemed to have grown younger in the past few days. His feet knocked against the chair legs without reaching the floor and he was impossibly thin, his skin almost transparent, the veins traceable rivers in his arms. Between tentative bites of a cold roast beef sandwich, he told John that Marianne was upset because government men were digging up the garden. John tried to remember if there had been anything in the contracts about preserving the lawn.

"Where's Mummy now?"

"Gone for a walk." Philip handed him the note Marianne had written in his geography copybook. He read the looping scrawl of his wife's handwriting. It was clearer than usual, a little more carefully written, as a concession to her son. John had been bending down to understand better what Philip was saying and now his muscles hurt as he stood. "Try to eat that up, we'll have something nice tomorrow."

He drove the half mile or so up to the big house. Parking the car at the back, on the patch of grass in front of the barn, he took a shortcut through the scullery door. In the kitchen, the chessboard tiles had just been washed, so he walked on his tip-

toes across them, leaving a crescent trail behind. He unlocked
the front door and deliberately left it swinging open behind him.
He would have to talk to Murphy about this. Dulough was never
locked.

First he would take a look at the grass. They had indeed
dug up the lovely old stone path, and remnants of it had been
thrown here and there. Underneath, there was a small stream
that originated somewhere behind the house and headed for the
sea. He hadn't known about it and wondered why the first gardeners had thought to cover it up. It seemed a pity. Picnics on
the lawn had been a specialty of his mother's. He remembered
lying on the blanket as she put out the tea things. The children
drank very milky tea (the milk quotient decreased as one got
older, until, at fifteen or sixteen, it was the same color as the
adults'). Their mother always insisted that they wait an hour before they went swimming—she was petrified they would get a
cramp. When she gave the all clear, he and Phil ran down to
the beach and raced each other to the island and back, while
their mother watched from the shore, towels at the ready. John
couldn't fathom why his children liked the pool better; as far as
he was concerned, nothing could beat sea-bathing.

Marianne would be in her new garden, hiding from the
mess down here. As he climbed up through the forest to the
flat piece of land on the other side, he felt an anticipation at
seeing her, after his final meeting with Foyle. He wondered
whether he should explain why he'd lied to her the day before.
If he put it in the right terms, she'd understand. But surely
she should understand without him having to say anything, he
thought.

It was late afternoon. She was on her knees at the edge of a flower bed, heaping soil around a new planting. He stopped on the ridge, watching. She wasn't wearing her gardening clothes but a skirt, which she had pulled up over her knees so as to keep it clean. He wondered what she could have been doing that day to require a skirt. She would be cold. He had meant to go straight to her, to comfort her about the lawn, but when she gave the soil a final pat and stood up, she turned her back to him and looked out to sea. She *was* cold, he could see that now, in the stiff way that she moved. He thought how seldom it was that he had a chance to watch Marianne, how different his wife seemed when she thought she was alone. Without taking her eyes off the sea, she squatted on the ground. Then she began to rock back and forth. The act was unfamiliar to John, and disconcerting in its inelegance. He wondered what she could be doing. And then the obviousness of it hit him, his own stupidity! She was crying, of course.

He had wanted to tell her about his afternoon, and how Mrs. Baskin said she was going to come up to the house one of these days to "have a look at the place." But he stepped back into the undergrowth. It was dark in the forest, the light outside too weak to penetrate. He slipped down the paths, his hands grabbing at tree trunks until he was at the bottom.

When she came back, it was getting dark and he had begun supper. He had not been particularly successful in the beginnings of this impromptu meal and was glad to see her. There was not a speck of mud on her skirt, nor was there any evidence of her distress. She smiled at Philip, who was helping with dinner.

"Did you see the stream, Mummy?" he said, as he led her to the kitchen table, where his and Kate's drawings of the valley were laid out side by side. Kate arrived at the kitchen door, settling against the frame.

As Marianne hugged Philip, she watched John over the top of the child's head. He could feel it as he opened and closed cupboards, which made him wonder if she had sensed him watching her hours earlier. No, he had been well hidden, and besides, he was expecting her disapproval; she would blame him for the lawn, for the stone path, he knew this. What would she say when she found out the full extent of his agreement with the government, that they had almost no power over what happened at Dulough now?

Philip

Philip slipped out of the cottage and made his way up the avenue towards the big house and, beyond it, to the beach. He carried a shovel that he'd taken from Francis's work shed. It thumped off the ground, sending shock waves into his shoulder. He was beginning to regret taking the stupid thing and he wondered if he should leave it behind the hedge. It would be difficult to come back for it when the tide came in, though.

The government car, which always seemed to be parked in front of the house these days, had not yet arrived. He was pleased to know that he'd got the better of them. Turning, he went under the archway that was the entrance to the garden. He checked on the stream he'd fixed; the water flowed smoothly, straightly down to the sea. It was clearer now that the earth had settled, now that the worms and cigarette butts had been washed away. He scooped a handful into his mouth. It tasted of rust.

Pushing his way between the pines at the foot of the lawn, he arrived at the top of the cliffs. The headland curled away to his left and right like crab claws, peninsulas that belonged to his family but were never used. They were too near the sea for the deer, and the ground wasn't good enough to grow anything other than rough grass. Owen Mór had once asked Philip's father if he could put his sheep there. His father had said yes but retracted his offer when Francis convinced him that it wasn't a good idea, that the animals would get in and ruin the gardens. Francis didn't much like Owen Mór, because his blue-daubed sheep had a habit of jumping in front of the car on the way to town.

Philip went down the winding sandy path. It was steep, and he used the shovel to steady himself. The tide was out, leaving behind seawater-filled rivulets on the sand and a few jelly-fish, their tentacles plastered to the beach, dying slowly. Philip stopped to look at one; it lay half in, half out of a pool. There was no sign that it was alive, but he wasn't sure how to tell. Did jellyfish breathe? Lifting the spade as high as he could, he cut the creature in two. It was like slicing through trifle, each side stayed intact, nothing spilled out, no blood and guts, it just wobbled for a moment and was still. In fact, unless you looked at it closely, you couldn't even see that it had been cut in half at all. Philip brought the spade down again and cut it into quarters, then into eighths, clearly, symmetrically, as if he was drawing a mathematical diagram. To finish the job, he severed the tentacles where they met the body. He imagined the water coming in and lifting it, intact at first, then separate, each piece floating off in a different direction, on the tide.

As he walked on, he looked back a couple of times, but he couldn't distinguish his jellyfish from the others now. The water was still a long way out when he reached the slippery rocks that formed the base of the island. They were covered in bladder-wrack; the oily sacks popped under his feet. He slowly climbed up to where the baby mussels were, the only surface with a decent foothold.

When he and Kate came out here with their parents, his father told him that Philip the First had made the flagstone path that wound from the rocks to the chapel. Philip the First was his ancestor, the one who'd built Dulough. Philip's father always said "PhiptheFirst" as if it were one word. He would chuckle afterwards, amused at making him sound like one of the kings of England. His father took particular care to tell *him* stories about Philip the First, as if he would be more interested because they shared a name. As a result, this Philip was much better versed in the history of Dulough than his sister.

The path was overgrown, and some of the flagstones had broken in two where the roots pushed up underneath. The church had been built right in the center of the island, but now it was imperceptibly nearer the far end, as the waves that crashed against the seaward side slowly eroded the rocks. Through neglect, and because of the battering it got from the wind and rain, the church had fallen derelict. The roof was long gone, and grass grew amongst the rotting carcasses that were the pews, pushing up through the cracks in the floor. There had been a stained glass window at the landward end of the church, but the glass had never been there in Philip's time. His father said that he barely remembered it himself, that it had blown out in a big storm when he was a little boy. The family had been quite glad of it, actually. They had grown tired of taking the boat out on Sunday mornings, and the local minister really hadn't the time to fit such a small, inaccessible congregation into his rounds.

The only object that had stayed perfectly unchanged was the white marble altar, which had been planted parallel to the shore, at the top of the aisle. Philip stood in front of it now, holding his shovel. He was wondering where to build his hut. If he built it inside the church, he would have the advantage of having one ready-made wall—two, if it was in a corner. But he wasn't sure about the idea. He wasn't sure if it was right to build a hut in a church, even a derelict one, and it would be more difficult to hide it if anyone should come out to the island. No, he would have to make it at the far end, where not even Francis would go.

He went out through the door shaped like a bishop's hat and into the churchyard. It was still used by the family. Though one of Francis's jobs was to pull the weeds away from the graves, they grew with a ferocity that no one could keep pace with. Philip's father had suggested that it wouldn't be a bad idea to let Owen Mór's sheep loose out there for a while, but Francis refused to entertain that notion either.

The place was wild with grass; it was knee-high on the path, it grew in clumps at the foot of the headstones, it sprouted from the granite slabs on top of the graves, though there was no soil to sustain it there. Moss and lichen covered the headstones, so that the lettering had become barely legible. This Philip's father said that one of these days they should bring out paper and charcoal to do a rubbing, before the words were lost forever.

A ring of yew trees encircled the churchyard, a sign that his family believed they were going to heaven. But the trees had the opposite effect. It was dark under their canopy, even in the middle of the day. The roots curled themselves into the graves and the branches twisted into the contortions of the wind. Philip had been told to never, ever eat their berries, that he'd be dead in minutes. He wasn't quite sure he believed it.

He wandered amongst the stones, running a hand along the lettering, the lichen rough and staining his fingers. The church-yard wasn't even a quarter full. Though his family had been buried there for a century and a half, there was room, by his calculations, for another four hundred and fifty years' worth of Campbells. He wondered whether the island would still be here then. He had learnt in geography that it had been created mil-lennia ago, and that it would probably be around for at least another thousand years. In that case, there wasn't enough room for all the Campbells who would live at Dulough after this Philip. He walked over to his grandparents' grave; they were buried by the low drystone wall that marked the divide between holy and unholy ground. His father had tried to explain the dif-ference between places you could bury people and places you couldn't. For example, you couldn't just bury someone in the garden, you had to put them in ground that had been conse-crated by the church. His grandparents' grave was the newest and best looked after; they had the same headstone. His other grandparents were still alive; they lived in Dublin.

Sticking the spade into the ground, he looked out to sea. It was a gesture he'd seen Francis perform many times on the mainland. He was glad to be rid of the weight of the shovel, the awkwardness of it. He looked about for a good place to start building. It was difficult to find a level piece of ground, and one that had a decent view of the house; he wanted to be able to watch the comings and goings when the tourists arrived. Fi-nally, he began clearing a patch of brambles and thistles; their roots went deep into the earth and he had to be content with lopping them off at ground level rather than pulling them out altogether.

He stamped the remaining roots down and threw out the small stones littering his den, clearing a space roughly the size of his old window ledge. Were any of the government people in his room now? he wondered. Looking up at the house, he couldn't see any activity from here, but his room was at the back anyway. He told himself that he'd have this to come to instead, when it was properly finished. But he wasn't sure how to go about constructing a hut that would withstand the elements; the sea winds and the Donegal rain beat the island hardest of all. The walls would have to be stone, there was no doubt about that; if he built them out of anything else—wood, say, or clods of earth—there'd be nothing left the next time he came. There were enough drystone walls on the island, built in Philip the First's time, for him to plunder. He knew that he shouldn't do that; his father had told him that drystone wall making was an ancient art. But if his father hadn't decided to open Dulough to the public, he wouldn't have needed to take the stones.

Philip wondered what time it was and whether the green car and the white van had arrived yet. What did they do every day, the people from the government? He imagined them sitting around, drinking endless cups of tea on the camp chairs in the drawing room, and Mrs. Connolly in the kitchen, exasperated. When they introduced themselves around the place, the man with the moss-colored suit said that they were "overseeing the transition from private to public." Philip understood each word, but he wasn't quite sure what they meant together.

He began dismantling the wall furthest away from the church, the one he thought would be missed least. The stones were lighter than he expected, and he lifted them easily into a pile where the hut was going to be. He had watched the men digging foundations for the cottage and wondered whether he should dig them here too. But he could barely pull the roots out of the ground, let alone get a spade into it. Instead, he laid the bigger stones around the edge of the space he'd cleared so that they fitted together like a puzzle. It took a while; he was getting hungry. The sun was well up; it must have been breakfast time or later. He wished he had brought something to eat. Digging around in the pockets of his anorak, he found a Fox's Glacier Mint that his father had given him on one of their walks. The wrapper was stuck to the sweet and it took him a while to peel it off. But he was glad of the feeling of something in his mouth—it was certainly better than those cold meat sandwiches. He wondered if that was the way things would be now that Mrs. Connolly had no time to cook for them. These days, she was always up at the house, getting things ready for the visitors. She would be making afternoon teas with scones and cream and jam for them. And there'd be Coke. Usually they weren't allowed Coke, but now he would be able to have it whenever he liked. Aside from living next door to Francis, that was the other good thing to come out of all this.

Wiping his nose with the back of his hand, the mint finished, he went on with the wall. He realized that he would only be able to build it as big as he was; he had no ladder to go any higher. Tomorrow he'd bring out books, a torch, and some food. He would need to find a tin to keep his things dry. And he wondered where he might find a piece of old carpet to cover the earth.

There was some warmth in the sun now; he decided that it

must be late morning. He would need to get back before the tide cut him off completely. The water was still quite far away, but he knew that this was deceptive; you thought you'd lots of time and then suddenly the sea was knee-deep and you had to sling your shoes over your shoulders to wade back. The hut would have to be finished tomorrow, but he was happy with the progress he'd made. The wall was at least waist-high. He shoved little stones into the cracks to make it even sturdier. It was almost as good as one of Francis's.

His eye caught a movement on the mainland. Someone had come to the end of the garden. Philip tried to make out who it was. It had to be either his father or his mother—or Francis; Mrs. Connolly would not leave the kitchen for a walk at this hour. He supposed it could be one of the gardeners or the people from the government, but they always traveled in packs. It was impossible to make out from this distance whether the figure was male or female. The only thing he could tell for sure was that they were looking out to sea; he could see the smear of paleness that was the face. He considered waving. He had had enough now and was eager to come back. But the hut was to be a secret, and he knew that whoever it was would want to know what he'd been doing on the island since very early that morning. Instead, he stayed still, hoping he blended into the darkness of the sea behind him. Soon the figure turned and vanished back into the trees.

As Philip emerged at the top of the cliff, carrying Francis's spade, he was thinking about his hut and the things he would do to it tomorrow, what he would need to bring out with him at low tide. He wouldn't want the shovel anymore, but he could do with a hammer and some nails if he was to make the roof out of wood. He wondered if Francis was noticing his tools going missing. Where would he find some decent, wide planks, ones with varnish on them so that they wouldn't rot?

He had intended to wash off the spade, which was caked in earth and sand, in the stream he'd mended. But when he went to dip the blade in the water at the bottom of the cliff, it was dirty again. The same men as before, the ones whose cigarettes he'd taken, were placing large concrete blocks over his stream, like a bridge. A small cement mixer stood, churning, and sinking into the lawn, a few feet away from them. Both had their backs to him as they maneuvered a particularly large block into place. He was too close to turn around without being seen, so he sauntered past with the shovel, as if he was on his way to do some work of his own. The men dropped the block and turned to look. The one with the sailor's cap said, "They're searching for you up at the house," as he pulled a packet of cigarettes out of his breast pocket. They were John Player Blues. Philip remembered the damp, smoky taste in his mouth. Who was looking for him up at the house? The people from the government? Had they found out that he'd been in his old room? He thought about the man who hadn't flinched when Mrs. Connolly poured tea on the back of his hand. He wouldn't have much tolerance for children who didn't do what they were told. Philip imagined the man pouring teapot after teapot onto his outstretched hands. And him not being allowed to flinch, either.

"Your mother thinks you've been eaten by the sharks," the other man added.

Both men grinned, as if they too had had mothers who'd fussed over their whereabouts at one time or another. Philip smiled shyly at them, relieved that it was only his mother and not the man in the green suit who was looking for him.

But she had been watching from the upstairs drawing room and had seen him emerge through the trees at the end of the lawn. Now, as he stood by the two workmen, he saw her striding across the grass. He thought about the figure who had come to the edge of the cliff and looked out to sea; he matched it now to his mother in her old coat and gardening trousers. The pale smear in the distance had been her face, scanning the horizon for his. The men slid their cigarettes back into their pockets again and busied themselves with another one of the massive blocks. She smiled at them and nodded, but Philip noted that it was not one of her better smiles.

"I was digging for worms." He stuck close to the men.

"Since the crack of dawn?" Her voice rose at the end, frightening him.

He could see that she was very angry, much angrier than she'd been when she discovered the lawn ruined. She put a lock of hair that had fallen from her ponytail behind her ear. Her hair, Philip thought, was like pigeon's feathers, silvery at the front and dark at the back. She took him by the shoulder and moved him away from the men. Bending down to look into his face, she said, "Where are they then?"

For a moment, Philip couldn't think what she was talking about, and then he realized that she meant the worms. "I let them go."

He knew that it was an absurd response, that no one went digging for lugworms and then put them back. His mother looked at him intently and he saw himself reflected in her eyes, small and puny, as he'd been in the upstairs drawing room mirror on the day of the move. Her right hand, extended, gripped his shoulder so that her nails dug in. He could see that she didn't realize that she was hurting him; all her concentration rested on his face, on trying to read where he had really been. But she gave up and rose slowly, as if she were an old woman, older than Mrs. Connolly.

Later, when he'd locked her out of his new room, he took off his shirt; there was a nick in the hollow of his collarbone, where her thumb had pushed in too hard. He got into bed with his shoes on, the mud dirtying the sheets. It would serve her right.

John

John's study was a round room in the turret, the hinge to Du-lough's wings; besides the kitchen, it was the only room to have kept its furniture through the move. The first Philip's tartan, a predictable dark forest green inlaid with blue, lined the walls from floor to ceiling. Above the fireplace was a set of deer antlers and on the mantelpiece, a King James Bible, brought over from Scotland. It was almost a foot thick. The Campbell births and deaths were recorded on the flyleaf. John had dutifully added Kate's and Philip's names when they were born.

A couple of days before the move, Mr. Murphy had found him here. He knocked before coming in and seating himself opposite.

"Could I have a quick word?" He always behaved like a houseguest who worried that he was overstaying his welcome, rather than the person who was in charge of the estate now. "Mr. Foyle and I were wondering whether you'd be willing to write a history of Dulough?" He paused. "For the visitors. We'll be handing out a brochure on the first day. I'm going to ask your wife if she'll write something about the gardens, too, so that they'll know what's what."

John smiled. He'd thought that perhaps he was going to have his study taken away from him after all.

Before he could answer, Murphy added, "Foyle wanted to write it himself, but I talked him out of it. I want the insider's take. It doesn't have to be too long." Murphy got up to leave, the chair creaking beneath him. "The thing is to give the visitors something to get their teeth into." He rested his hand on the doorknob for a couple of seconds. "A good story. The sort of thing they'd want to hear about a place like this."

John had spent much of the week since the move wondering what Michael had meant by that. He knew the bare bones of the family's history—and there were Olivia Campbell's diaries from the eighteen hundreds: copious, often sentimental, writings about life on the estate, nothing to whet the appetites of tourists eager for a slice of colonial intrigue.

How did one begin something like this? How could he make people interested in Dulough? *Du-lough: Du, a corruption of the Irish word* dubh, *black, and* lough, *lake. The estate is called Du-lough, or, in English, Black Lake, because of the depth of the water which filled this glaciated valley after the last ice age.*

Dulough was built between 1854 and 1857 by Philip Campbell. No, that was the way one expected a thing like this to begin. He needed to think of something more attention-grabbing: *In 1854, a tyrannical, rich Scottish landowner by the name of Philip Campbell*...Was it in his interest to call his own ancestor tyrannical?

Philip and Olivia Campbell arrived in Ireland in the spring of 1852, not long after the Famine, when the frost was beginning to thaw in the cold, unforgiving valley of Dulough. Philip was looking to expand his vast Scottish holdings and he had heard that the barren land of north Donegal, which looked so much like his own country, was going cheap.

The Campbells had already spent a month visiting the milder climes of Wicklow, Wexford, and Kerry. Olivia found Wicklow particularly beautiful and legend has it that she tried to per-suade her husband to buy there. But he was determined on his bargain, and they came north—in April, when the southern counties are experiencing spring showers but Donegal has not yet shed the pall of winter.

Campbell wanted a vast tract of land, a piece that would both complement and rival his Scottish estates. It was a local priest who suggested Dulough; its steep valley and bottomless lake were just what the gentleman was looking for. The priest's motives were altruistic; he had watched his flock suffer through the Famine and knew that in order for Campbell to establish his grand estate, he would need to buy out several small struggling families who could make nothing of the rocky soil and would be much better off living somewhere else.

The three families who owned their land jumped at Camp-bell's offer, but the priest had forgotten to mention that there were at least five who rented and that he would inherit them as tenants. Once the deal was done, Campbell contracted his cousin, Charles Wrenn-Harris, an architect from Edinburgh, to draw up plans for a house. He also, in the autumn of 1854, set about evicting the remaining tenant families from his land, claiming that their rent was in arrears. A local reporter de-

*scribed Campbell's men removing the families and their posses-
sions from their cottages and nailing the front doors shut (later
that morning a rudimentary battering ram would make them
uninhabitable). But of course nothing could be done. Ireland
was still a part of the British Empire; the law did not favour the
destitute.*

The ruins of those cottages and the ridges where the families
had grown potatoes—without much luck—were visible in the
foothills of the valley. There was one family left in town, the
O'Callaghans, whose ancestors had been evicted. John's father
had begun to lease them a couple of Dulough's better fields
at far below market value when he took over the estate. John
had stopped charging them rent altogether when his turn came.
When his accountant asked about it, he couldn't bring himself
to tell the truth, claiming that the land went unused. When he
saw the O'Callaghans in town he avoided them, as he imagined
they did him. Murphy would find out about the arrangement
soon enough and put a stop to it, no doubt.

*Once Campbell had rid himself of his tenants, he began work
on the house in earnest. He chose a naturally flat promontory
on the lake, with excellent views of the valley and, in the
distance, the sea. To his cousin, Campbell gave obsessive instructions: The house must be grand enough to impress any
friends he and Olivia might invite to stay with them, but not
so grand as to offend his Presbyterian sensibility. This delicate
balance consumed Campbell and Wrenn-Harris as they drew
and redrew the plans. Finally a house that was elegantly in
keeping with the stark beauty of the valley, but devoid of any*

luxuries, was born. Visitors may be interested to note that all the bathrooms are without mirrors and instead have windows above the basins, so that the bather may worship God's beauty rather than their own.

And yet, though my ancestor planned meticulously, he was seized by a stab of conscience during the building of the house. Much to his cousin's dismay, he halted construction before Dulough was complete; the ballroom on the third floor went unfinished. His cousin felt that Campbell's decision was a mutilation of his design, and the two were never to speak again.

The house was not the sole building erected by Campbell. In tandem, the chapel on the island was built. Thousands of years ago, a part of the demesne collapsed into the sea, leaving an island that is now less than a mile square. Campbell very much liked the idea that it would take physical hardship for his family to worship, that they would have to walk out over the sand to the island or, when the tide was in, take a boat. The chapel was spared no expense; though there were never more than a few congregants, it was equipped for up to a hundred. The design, both inside and out, is quite traditionally Gothic, but simplified for Philip's tastes. He and Olivia are buried there, as is every family member since. We regret that the island will not be open to visitors.

When he was satisfied with the house, Campbell set about designing the gardens. Here he could do as he liked, as he could be sure that the more exotic his planting was, the more pleased his God would be. (Please see my wife's guide for a more detailed description of the grounds.)

In 1863, when the gardens were still in their infancy, Philip Campbell took ill. Though his illness went undiagnosed at the time, his symptoms suggest a cancer of the respiratory system. He died quickly, and by autumn Olivia Campbell was mistress of Dulough.

Olivia was a thoroughly different character to her late husband and set about modifying the estate to her own tastes. I have no doubt that, had she been able to find them, she would have restored the evicted families to their homes. At forty, she was still a comparatively young woman and, rather surprisingly, she was not intimidated by the estate's isolation. After selling off much of her husband's land in Scotland, she made Dulough her home. Photographs from the years after his death show elaborate picnics in the gardens and parties in the swimming bath by the lake. She became a patroness of the arts, using her wealth to establish scholarships in the local secondary school, as well as inviting both British and Irish artists to stay and work at Dulough.

But Olivia enjoyed the friendship of one artist in particular, Geoffrey Roe, who bought the guesthouse at Lough Power, where the Campbells had stayed all those years before. His great-grandson, the well-known sculptor Edward Steele, lives at Lough Power today.

Though Olivia is keen to point out in her diaries that she never attended Roe's parties, she did come to know him well. He was a great contrast to her first husband: Where Philip was religious, Roe was a known atheist, widely reported to have left London after a string of soured affairs. Where Philip took pride in denying the self, Roe was famous for doing just as he pleased. He is very often in her writings, easel set towards the sea, troubling some servant or other for a jar of water for his brushes, or a rag, or a gin and tonic.

Once, in a London gallery, John had seen a painting by Geoffrey Roe tucked into an exhibition entitled Water Women. There, between two of Bonnard's paintings of Marthe in the bath, was a picture called *C. Bathes*. It was significantly less accomplished than Bonnard's, and Roe would never have been shown alongside such a master had his subject matter not fit the theme of the exhibition. The perspective of *C. Bathes* was from the woman's head; the face itself wasn't visible, the body almost submerged. It was modest compared to the paintings surrounding it. The date and location were listed as unknown, but John recognized the bathroom as Dulough's, and knew instantly that the "C" stood for Olivia Campbell.

The Campbells had just one child, Duncan, a solicitor in Edinburgh. Olivia bought an apartment in the New Town and visited him regularly, but after one such visit, she wrote in her diary that she was 'always happy to return to Dulough' (3 June 1878) and that she feared that, after her death, her son would 'neglect the house and gardens, leaving them in the hands of some caretaker or other, never bothering to visit himself' (5 November 1880). She eventually chose to leave the estate to my great-grandfather Thomas Harvey, her sister's child, adding the stipulation that their first son must be christened Philip and that the owner of the house must always be named Campbell.

Olivia died in 1910. Unlike her husband, she was much mourned by the local community. Thomas Harvey arrived the following year from England with his wife, Sarah, to take over the running of Dulough. They brought my grandmother Caroline with them. She was ten. Though Olivia indicated that her diaries were to be burnt, the Harveys found them a great handbook to the workings of the estate; there were notes on the house's quirks, how to treat particular blights in the gardens, how to go about pruning a rhododendron, which butcher to trust—and which of the regular guests had outstayed their welcome.

My grandmother Caroline was twenty-two when the Civil War exploded in Ireland. The IRA were roaming the country, torching the big houses of the Anglo-Irish. Dulough was an obvious target because of my ancestor's cruelty to the tenant farmers so soon after the Famine. At that time, Caroline wrote:

'I woke suddenly this morning. It was still dark & I had a feeling that something was different—or not quite right. I put my dressing-gown on & went out into the hall. It was silent; I couldn't hear the wind anymore. There was a creak on the stairs & before I had time to be afraid, I saw Daddy disappearing into his study. I knocked on the open door. His gun rested against the desk, the barrel pointing up to the ceiling. It was the first time I'd seen it out of the locked cabinet in the hall. "Caroline, you understand what's happening, that Ireland is in great trouble at the moment?" I told him that I understood it very well & that the English should get out and leave us to our own devices. My father smiled and said, "Unfortunately our position is not quite that simple, although I agree that Ireland should be left to its own devices, as you put it." I waited for him to elaborate, but instead, he turned and looked out the window.'

In this extract, we can see that my great-grandfather felt the threat to Dulough was very real indeed. And yet the Irish Republican Army didn't burn the house as they had burnt so many others (perhaps we were simply too far north). But, a few months later, a group of local men, claiming to be the local *faction of the IRA, marched down the avenue and up to the front door. They knocked politely and informed the housekeeper that they would be taking over Dulough 'as long as it served the needs of the Irish people.' The housekeeper informed them that they would not, and that she recognised more than a few of them. This tactic was successful in diminishing the invasion but not in stopping it completely, and a small group of young men who would have been much more at home in the fields than fighting for the needs of the Irish people used the dining room as a Center of Operations for a few months in the winter of 1922/3. The occupation ended when the family became tired of eating in the kitchen, and when my grandmother formed a strong friendship with a quiet local boy, my great-grandfather informed them that Dulough had more than played its part in the fight for independence.*

For a time, Dulough was silent again after the IRA occupation. My grandmother missed the boyish IRA contingent terribly. So she was thrilled when she won a scholarship to Trinity College in Dublin to read Physics, a very unusual subject for women to study then. Upon graduation, she married my grandfather George Monk, of Enniskerry, Co. Wicklow, the son of close family friends. The price he paid for the estate was his name. He promptly became 'George Campbell', at least on paper.

My father, Philip the Second, was born in 1933 and was to be their only child. He married my mother, Katherine, in 1956, and my brother, the third Philip, was born in June of 1958. I came along two years later. I have happy memories of my childhood. Until we went to boarding school, we had lessons in the mornings, taught by both my father and my mother in the up-

stairs drawing room. When we had finished our school-work, we had a lot to occupy us; I remember building a tree house in one of the oaks by the avenue, the remains of which are still visible today.

My brother went to Trinity to study law when I was fifteen, making it clear that I would have the responsibility of taking over Dulough when the time came.

Surely that was enough. He massaged the web of skin between his right thumb and forefinger. There they were, fiction and truth, so tightly bound that minutes after writing them, he could almost forget which was which. It had come more easily than he had expected. Turning to the first page, he wrote *Dulough: The History of a House in Donegal*. He scratched it out: *Dulough: The History of a Donegal House*. No. *Dulough: A History*. He knew now that the house would never be lived in again, that he'd put something in motion that couldn't be reversed. Perhaps they all thought it was a good thing—the Campbells were blow-ins who'd turfed five families out of their homes; it was only right that locals should be able to lounge around his house now, having tea and scones on the patio.

He thought about Kate and Philip, how his son had to carry on that name, a word whose short "L" suggested him perfectly, a little slip of a thing, but also that first Philip and his cruelty. What sort of future had he made for them; what damage had he done them? And his wife. Having watched her crying up there in her garden when she thought no one was looking, he knew she wasn't happy. The exhilaration he'd been getting from writing about the estate vanished. He wanted to have it finished now.

I followed my brother to Dublin three years later, but geography was my subject. I met my wife, Marianne, there. Upon graduating, we married in the chapel on the island. We have two children, Katherine and Philip.

We very much hope that you enjoy your visit and that you will return.

As he was contemplating whether he should sign his name at the end, Marianne appeared at the door. He wondered how long she'd been there, with that disapproving look on her face, watching him labor over the house's history. He knew she found it unfair that he got to keep his study when Philip was so upset at having lost his room. "Can't talk now," he said, fixing his gaze firmly back on his work, determined not to look up again until she was gone. He sensed her weight shift and her body turning away. Why couldn't she understand that he needed to keep his study—and that Philip had a perfectly good bedroom in the cottage?

When he was quite sure she was gone, that she was too far away to hear anything, he went over to the fireplace and picked up a vase with an elaborate pattern on it. He knew it was valuable. Lifting it over the hearth, as high as his chest, he let it go. It crashed onto the tiles, cracking one neatly down the middle, and broke into smithereens. It was so quiet in the house that the breaking sound hung in the air. He stayed still until it stopped.

But he found, as he lay in bed that night, that he didn't have it in him to cope with a battle on two fronts. The following morning, in the moments after they woke, when he hoped her guard was down, he said, "Let's go to Dublin for the weekend. Mrs. Connolly can look after the children."

She surprised him. "Yes," she said simply, as she pulled on her dressing gown. She must have thought that they needed it very badly if she was agreeing to leave Kate and Philip behind, so he suggested that they didn't stay with her parents, that they stay in a proper hotel, in town, and go for nice meals. He would phone the Shelbourne.

They stopped in Enniskillen for a pub lunch of toasted sandwiches and half-pints of lager. As they passed through the border, they talked of an event that had now long passed into family lore, the time that John's father had driven through a checkpoint within an hour of a bomb, how he'd been watching the news that night and there it was, the tower blown sky-high, the pieces strewn about the field, amongst the cows. The soldiers he'd offered sweets to probably dead. Or maybe not. He'd chosen to believe that the one he'd chatted with as they'd checked over his car, as they'd opened the boot and rifled through its contents, who, by the sound of him, was from Cornwall, or Devon or one of those lovely southern English counties, hadn't been killed.

John calculated how much their lunch would cost with the exchange rate, the Irish pound weak against the British. But perhaps this would help them when they opened the gates to the visitors, perhaps it would bring the Northerners to Donegal. He was counting on the Americans, though. They were more susceptible to the myth.

The way into Dublin looked quite different, with its vast new spiderweb of roads.

"Do you think that you could have a look at the map, perhaps? Find out where we went wrong?" John asked Marianne.

"Oh yes, sorry—course." She unclicked her seat belt and climbed into the backseat to rummage about. Most people her age would have twisted around, felt for the map with one hand, but Marianne threw herself into things—scrambled up mountains, ran down to the sea. It was one of her most endearing qualities, John thought, and it was one of the many that made her a much better parent than he was.

When they arrived at the hotel, Marianne's excitement at the journey had abated and she seemed angry again. Dropping their bags, he looked out the window. "We have a wonderful view of the green."

She disappeared into the bathroom; he heard the water running. Closing their bedroom door as quietly as he could, he went down to the lobby to phone Mrs. Connolly. She sounded harried. He knew that she felt that they'd asked too much of her, that she had enough to do in the run-up to the opening. But the children would be no bother at all.

In the hotel bar, he ordered a drink. It was best to leave Marianne to her own devices; she would come to find him when she was ready. He looked out the window. The people were rich, there was no other word for it, with their expensive clothes and hands full of shopping. He saw Brown Thomas bags often. Even the bags themselves looked as if they'd cost a fortune to produce. They might assume that he was rich, too, sitting there in the bar of the Shelbourne, but the price of the hotel was out of their league. He'd have to put the bill on his credit card, reasoning with himself that he'd be getting a proper salary soon; he would pay it off.

Marianne came in wearing a long velvet skirt and a cardigan with Christmassy baubles hanging from it. John had never really enjoyed Marianne's dress sense, and yet the individuality of it was one of the things that had drawn him to her at college. Her hair was newly washed and she wore makeup; there was a sheen to her lips. She looked fresh, as if she had scrubbed off Donegal in the bath and was ready to become part of the city again.

"So, shall we go?" She landed, smiling, in the chair opposite. "Two drinks in one day, not like you." She took a sip of his Scotch. "Horrible stuff."

She was not usually this way. He found her shifting moods disconcerting. It was a symptom of the move, of upheaval, of the fact that he'd let her down. He should take advantage of her good humor now. Standing up, he offered her his arm.

They crossed the road so that they could walk along by Stephen's Green. Marianne reached up and touched various leaves, holding them between her fingers contemplatively and then letting them go so that they snapped back into place. She didn't say whether she approved of the gardeners' work or not.

John wanted to walk straight down Dawson Street to Trinity. He was not necessarily sentimental about his college days, but he always liked to visit when he was in town. Marianne never seemed interested in going back, though; she couldn't have been more eager to graduate, to move on to the next act of her life. She enjoyed being a mother much more than she'd ever liked being a student.

It was a busy Saturday and most people, with the exception of the groups of teenagers hanging limply around street corners, seemed to be in a great hurry. Some of them bumped into John without noticing; they would have apologized ten, or even five, years ago. It was all this new money, he thought—we're a different country now. But he knew that he was in no position to moralize; he had handed Dulough over to the government in order to make money.

That night, they took the bus to her parents' house in Rathmines. John wanted to drive, but Marianne said she missed public transport. Her father collected them from the bus stop and drove them the short distance home. The car was needlessly messy. John had to move a pile of books to get into the front seat and the floor was littered with newspapers and shopping bags.

"So you're finally getting rid of the place, then?" Patrick said as he put the car into gear.

"Well," John said, "I wouldn't . . ."

Marianne saved him. "No, Dad, the government's going to run the estate. We still own it."

Her father concentrated on the road. He chuckled. "Good to hear my grandchildren won't be homeless, then."

"No, they certainly won't be homeless." Annoyed, John added, "Anyway, the cottage is much more practical . . ."

Marianne reached over and patted his shoulder. He wasn't sure if that meant "It's all right" or perhaps "Calm down." But it was the first time she'd touched him since they'd arrived, and he was grateful for it.

Marianne had grown up in one of those red-brick terraced houses with large, uneven rooms and a gloomy kitchen on the bottom floor. Like their car, Patrick and Anna White's house was a mess. Every corner was filled: books, piles of sheet music, walking boots caked in mud, the dog's toys . . . It made John feel claustrophobic. He liked his parents-in-law on the whole, though. Patrick was a music teacher in a local secondary school and Anna always had a new project; she had just finished a bachelor's in modern Irish history. John saw textbooks on the floor by the back door.

His mother-in-law had Marianne's hair and, for that matter, Kate's, the little curly wisps around their faces. But Anna was thinner than Marianne, so thin that her wrists didn't look strong enough to hold the big dish she was lifting off the countertop. John took it out of her hands and laid it on the table.

"I'm afraid it's just pasta." She paused. "I would have cooked you something special if I'd known you were coming."

It wasn't a rebuke. One of the great blessings of John's marriage was that Patrick and Anna expected nothing of them. They weren't even offended when Marianne had told them they wouldn't be staying. In gratitude, John grasped Anna by the shoulders. He said teasingly, "How's the scholar of the family?"

"I graduated, wore the cap and gown and everything." She pointed to a photo on the fridge. He studied it. She was throwing her mortarboard in the air like a young woman.

"How are things up there?" She poured vinaigrette on the salad.

Both she and Patrick always referred to Donegal as if it were the North Pole. John was suddenly aware that Marianne and his father-in-law had deserted them and that they were alone in the kitchen. "Oh, you know." He wondered whether it would be enough to stave off Anna's enquiries.

"It can't be easy," she said.

Anna was one of those people who liked to talk about things. He was glad his own mother hadn't known her; they wouldn't have got on with each other at all.

"It must be hard on you, but it seems a very sensible decision to me. You'll have the best of both worlds, am I right? You won't have the worry of the maintenance."

He nodded glumly. "Shall I retrieve the others?" He told himself that she couldn't be expected to understand—that she'd never lived in a place like Dulough.

They took one of the last buses back into town. The daytime shoppers had become nighttime revelers. John and Marianne watched a young man lean a hand against a shop window and vomit onto the pavement. When he finished, he wiped his mouth and wandered back into a pub.

In their room, Marianne took her second bath of the day, more, she explained, because of the abundance of hot water than anything else. This time she left the bathroom door open. For a good ten minutes, John wondered whether he should go in or not. At last, he shoved his shoes under the bed and took the chance.

There was a towel rolled up under her head. The bubbles had all but melted and he could see the outline of her body under the water, her breasts and knees breaking the surface. He thought of that exhibition in London, of all those women, all those baths. She opened her eyes and smiled tiredly as he sat down on the loo seat. "Could you shut the door? It's a little chilly."

He got up silently, obligingly. She closed her eyes again. He wasn't sure when the balance of power had shifted. Was it when she'd had Kate? Was it when he'd signed the contract with the government? He hadn't been watching for it because he hadn't expected it. He tried to focus, to separate the years of their marriage, but he couldn't. It was one long, looping roll of film, the same images repeated again and again: house, garden, sea, children.

As he lifted his arm to reach down into the warm water, she got up suddenly and groped for a towel. Her eyes had been closed. She couldn't have seen his hand rising to touch her, but he wondered whether she had somehow sensed it, whether it was an indication for him to back away. He went into the bedroom and picked up the paper.

He woke before Marianne the next morning and, as he had done the day of the move, he quietly put on his clothes and slipped through the door. Outside, he headed for Stephen's Green. People crisscrossed it here and there, the early-morning workers of coffee shops and bakeries. Though it was early summer, they dug their hands into their jackets and sank down into their collars. Some were wrapped in scarves. Mostly women, they wore cheap coats and shoes. They had pale, unhealthy-looking skin, the undernourished pallor of Eastern Europeans. This was the new city workforce; like America, Ireland had become rich enough to need such people, who, he imagined, probably lived in tenements on the north side and sent money home. He wondered whether they wanted to stay or whether they were counting the days until they could leave. He couldn't think what the attractions of this modern Dublin were. To him it had changed for the worse. He could see that Marianne was invigorated by it, though, by the bursting shops and new cosmopolitanism, by the young Irish who looked, in contrast to the immigrants, healthy and confident.

He could have taken up the government's offer to buy Dulough right out from under them and they could have easily afforded a house in one of the better suburbs: Foxrock, Dalkey, Killiney. Or further out, in Wicklow—Enniskerry, perhaps, where he'd often stayed with his cousins on weekends away from college. But their beautiful old house had been sold years ago. He wondered briefly how they were.

If he'd sold Dulough, they could have sent Kate and Philip to a very good school, and if they had been careful, if he had invested wisely, he may not have had to work. But he had turned the government down. He hadn't told Marianne. Murphy thought he was crazy; he was incredulous when John handed back the piece of paper with the number on it, a very big number, money that reflected this new Ireland, a figure the likes of which John would never see again. At the time, he had been confident that Marianne would not have wanted him to take it, but now he wasn't so sure. It was too late anyway. The decision was made. They still owned Dulough and, in a city so full of immigrants, he was grateful that he'd held on to a house that told him who he was, rooting him firmly in his own country.

He rose up off the bench. The newsagent at the top of Grafton Street was pulling up its shutters. A girl set a sign outside: LOTTO JACKPOT! John had never played, but he'd seen many a local in Donegal scratching away at those little cards. He didn't even know how much it cost to buy a ticket. Grasping about for the notes in his pocket, he asked, "How does it work?"

The sales assistant explained it to him sympathetically, as if he were the foreigner and not her. He would have to choose a set of numbers and watch a television program. He left the counter to consider; the children's birthdays were an obvious choice, as was the year Dulough was built. He returned to the counter and received his ticket. On the walk back to the hotel he allowed himself to imagine what five million pounds could do for them; he could get the estate back and they'd never have to worry about money again. He closed his fingers around the ticket, securing it tightly at the bottom of his pocket.

When he got back to the hotel, the room was dark; it smelled unaired, mustily of sleep. He took off his shoes and slipped into bed beside Marianne, wrapping his arms around her waist. It reminded him of college. When he'd had early lectures, he would come back to find her sleeping in exactly this position, her knees pulled up to her chest, her hands gripping the covers tightly under her chin. She loved to sleep; even when they'd had the children it was he who had got out of bed more often than not, to bring them to her for feeding.

She clasped his hands within her own and pulled him in behind her. His knees locked with hers. It was too hot under the covers and he began to sweat. She drifted off again, but when she woke forty-five minutes later, she allowed him to touch her for the first time in months, to run his hands up her legs, to lift her long nightdress, to turn her towards him.

Philip

Philip had to abandon his hut for nearly a fortnight after his mother caught him coming up from the beach. He stayed mostly inside, arranging and rearranging his new room. The toys he'd played with before the move—his soldiers, his Technic Lego—seemed artificial now and required too much imagination compared to the real world of hut building. He wondered how he'd ever thought up battles and expeditions; he longed to go back out to the island.

Finally, he found a day when no one was around. He had read the *Irish Times* for the tides and watched from the top of the cliff as the sea was sucked away. He had two planks of wood with him, taken from Francis's shed, each with a layer of creosote to protect it from the rain. There was an urgency to get the hut finished now; he wouldn't be able to bring these things out once the visitors arrived.

Philip laid the planks across the roof; they were too long

and stuck out the sides. He crawled in. Barely any light came through the walls, he'd done a good job of filling the gaps between the big rocks with smaller stones and moss. He hadn't managed to find a piece of carpet, so he had covered the floor with leaves. Adding his coat to the pile, he lay down with his head towards the door, where the light was best. He propped himself up on his elbows and opened the tin he'd brought out with him today; it held a torch, a Famous Five book that his father had said he'd enjoyed when he was a boy, and some chocolate. He turned onto his back and shone the torch up at the ceiling. A spider, with a tiny body and eight long legs, ran across. He broke off a piece of chocolate, opened his book, and curled into a ball. He could hear the Atlantic in the distance, the waves crashing against the rocks. It would be better to live here than the cottage. Could he manage to spend the night without getting caught? If he went out when they'd all gone to sleep and came back very early in the morning, it might work. But if his mother had been that angry after he'd only been here for a few hours, he didn't like to think what she would do if she caught him out for a whole night.

The Famous Five wasn't very good; he'd have to find a different book for next time. On the way back, he knew better than to take the path that ran along the lawn, over his hidden stream. Instead, he climbed up into the forest. Huge ferns grew under the trees, moss clinging to their branches. Water dripped through everything. It was not an old forest, and very few of the trees and plants were native to Ireland. It had been planted by Philip the First. The paths were winding and thin and the undergrowth brushed your ankles as you walked. It was easy to get lost, to forget where the house was, whether the sea was behind

or in front of you. He wondered if the visitors would be allowed
to walk here. His mother had told him that there were only a
few places they weren't allowed to go: the new cottage, the Connollys' house, the kitchen of the big house, and the island. Mr.
Murphy, the man Mrs. Connolly had poured tea on, decided
this, she said. Since then Philip had been repeating these places
to himself in his head: their cottage, our cottage, the kitchen, the
island. Sometimes the words took on the rhythm of his footfalls
as he walked around; other times he matched them to songs he
knew, fitting them into the place where the old words had been.

To avoid the workmen, he had deliberately climbed up to the
highest point of the forest. Beginning his descent, he noticed
that little signs had been planted along the path. A long, thin
spike, with a green label at the top, named almost every plant
and tree. He bent down to look at one of them: *Pinus contorta*,
lodgepole pine. He knew the small slanted writing to be Latin,
but "lodgepole pine" seemed a funny name for the relatively
average-looking tree that sprouted high into the air above him.
On his way home, he read the labels, then pulled each one out
of the ground. When he reached the threshold of the forest, he
hid them all under a giant fern.

At the edge of the lawn, he almost tripped over a sign: WEL-
COME TO DULOUGH. PLEASE DO NOT WALK ON THE GRASS. He
stepped back onto the gravel. He thought of all the places he
wouldn't be able to go. But surely this didn't apply to him?
He lived here, he wasn't just a visitor, he knew how to walk
on the grass so as not to ruin it. Bending over, he tugged at
the sign, but it was much more substantial than the ones in
the forest and it wouldn't budge. He considered giving it a
good kick, but he was in open view of the drawing room win-

dow and he thought that it would be too risky. He walked off down the avenue, looking back at it from time to time.

When he got to the cottage, it was earlier than he expected. The kitchen clock said a quarter to five. There was no sound but the crackling of a roast in the oven. He couldn't believe it; they hadn't had a roast since before the move and even then it was only on Sundays. Today was Friday. He peered through the oven window and felt the intense heat on his eyelashes and nose. He looked for potatoes and carrots and parsnips; they were all there.

In every room objects from the big house were piled to the ceiling. By his parents' bed, a stack of old magazines reached over his head and a box of fine white china, wrapped in newspaper, was tucked in under his mother's dressing table. In their old room, her dressing table had always held the same configuration of perfumes and powders, but they had been swept to the side and an accordion file, jammed with papers, had taken the place of his mother's things.

He went over to the dresser and ran his finger down the paper accordion's edge. It made a sound like lots of little guns going off—*pap pap pap pap pap*. He did it again, more slowly this time, reading the labels as be went: Accounts, Bills, Children, Correspondence, Taxes. He supposed that "Children" meant him and Kate. He lifted the edge of that section and looked in. The note on top said: "Kate, IMMUNIZATIONS: measles, mumps, rubella, tetanus." He looked for a record of his own injections. It wasn't there.

He thought about all the barbed wire he'd cut fingers and shins on; you could get tetanus that way, from where the animals rubbed up against the fences. Could he have it now without knowing? Mrs. Connolly had had cancer. He remembered her going to Dublin to see the doctor there; she'd taken to her bed for a long time when she got back. There was a familiarity about the memory, as if it had happened very recently, but it hadn't; he had been younger, five or six, when she was sick. Then he realized what it was—Mrs. Connolly had not done the cooking while she was getting better and they'd had lots of horrible cold meals, like they were having now.

Shoving the record of Kate's injections back into the part that said "Children," he opened "Correspondence." Pulling out one of the letters, he held it up to the weak light. The type was faint, the paper onion-skin thin:

Dear Sir,

The Office of Public Works read your proposal with great interest. It is part of the mission statement of this organization to save the great houses of Ireland and to allow the Irish people to partake in the full enjoyment of them. We will be sending Mr. Michael Murphy from our Lifford office to inspect the property.

Yours sincerely,

John T. McGrath

The letter was repeated below in Irish, which Philip could recognize but not understand, except for *A Chara*, which he knew meant "Dear Friend." He looked at the date; the letter was more than three years old.

A door slammed. He put the letter back. But there was a smear of red along the edge of the file. He had cut himself and trailed blood over it. Jamming his finger into his mouth, he ran quietly to his room, listening to the sounds in the kitchen. It wasn't Kate because the opening and closing of cupboards was soft and measured. His sister banged things. Getting up off the bed, he went to the door and opened it a crack.

"I hear you, wee mouse." It was Mrs. Connolly. "Come out here and give me a hand."

He went into the kitchen, glad to see Mrs. Connolly, relieved that it wasn't his mother or father. Wearing her old blue house-dress and slippers with holes cut in the toes for her bunions, she bent over the oven and asked him what he'd been doing with himself.

"Not much," he said, suddenly overwhelmed with wanting to tell her about his hut. He knew he couldn't, though. Instead he asked her quietly, stupidly, "Is that for our dinner?"

Mrs. Connolly pushed the roasting tray back into the oven and turned to face him.

"It is. You could do with a good feeding." She pinched his side, pretending that there was no flesh to grab.

"Are we having it here?" Philip associated the cottage with picnicky food, the sort of stuff they'd been eating since the move, not with a roast, which, up at the big house, had always been served with a certain amount of ceremony. It would feel strange to have it at the cottage with the Leaning Tower of Pisa boxes, unwrapped china, and water marks on the floor.

Mrs. Connolly sat down slowly, her joints arthritic. Pulling out a second chair, she patted the table in front of it. She waited for him to sit too. "You'll be having all your meals down here from now on, *alannah,* you understand that, don't you?"

Philip nodded and waited for more, but there wasn't any.

Instead, Mrs. Connolly got up and opened the cutlery drawer.

"Now, we'll need to get the table set before the others come back wanting their dinner."

The table was set and Mrs. Connolly had gone next door to cook for Francis, leaving instructions with Philip as to when to turn off the oven. His mother and Kate arrived first, their faces flushed from the gardens; they had been labeling the trees and shrubs, they said, so that the visitors would know what they were. Philip's stomach fell; *they'd* been the ones sticking the little spikes into the ground. He'd assumed it was the gardeners.

"I looked for you," Kate said to Philip. "Where were you?"

Philip glanced at his mother, but she seemed to be busy taking off her boots and tucking her hair back into place in the mirror on the coatrack. He shrugged at Kate, who said, "You're always going off on your own these days."

"You'll be in very serious trouble if you go out to the island on your own again, do you understand me, Philip?"

So she had been listening. It was the second time in the space of an hour he'd been asked whether he understood something. "Yes," he felt like shouting, "YES!" But he knew that it would make her angry, so instead he said to himself, yes, yes, he understood, no dinners at the big house and no going to the island.

It had been half an hour since Philip turned off the oven, but the roast was still hot, and from time to time it let off a *crack!* as if to remind them that it was there and ready to be eaten. A few minutes earlier, Kate had let out a sigh and opened one cupboard after another, looking for something to eat while she waited. She found the end of a loaf in the bread bin and, without offering it to their mother or him, she began to gnaw on the corner. Philip knew that she was punishing him for his caginess about where he'd been that day and the days before, and that she was punishing their mother for making them wait for their father.

They were all starving by the time his father arrived back. It was a quarter to eight, much later than they usually had supper. The rain had blown through the door with him, adding another patch to the floor. "Hope that's not down for the weekend," he said, as he pulled off his boots, "or we'll be washed out of it tomorrow."

"You're very late, darling." And from her voice Philip could tell that she was scolding his father, but more gently than she would scold the children. His parents were always polite to each other.

"Am I?" He looked up at the kitchen clock. "Am I? Yes, I'm sorry, well, we're all here now, it's a celebration of sorts, I suppose."

His father put his hands on the back of Philip's chair. Philip could feel his breath and smell the wax emanating from his coat after the rain.

"Mrs. Connolly went to a lot of trouble. I hope it's not cold," his mother said.

It was then that his father understood that he'd held up dinner, that they'd all been sitting there waiting for him. "No, no, lovely," he said cheerfully, rubbing his hands together. "Shall I carve?"

He was relieved to see his father at the head of the table and his mother at the foot; there would at least be some resemblance to the ceremony of roast-eating up at the big house. Philip took great care in constructing his first bite, a little bit of meat and some potato covered in gravy. It hadn't got cold. Each of them, even his mother, ate quickly, as if they hadn't eaten in days and wouldn't eat again for a long time. No one spoke until their plates were empty. This was unusual because his parents disapproved of eating too fast, and both believed in the importance of good conversation at dinner.

There was silence as they sat back, stunned at how quickly they'd finished, at how long it had been since they'd had a decent meal. Then, as if he were about to make a toast, Philip's father pushed his chair back and stood up, his water glass raised. "As you all know," he paused and sat down again, "as you know, this is an important time for Dulough, which means it's an important time for us, too. There will be a lot of people here, which is going to feel very strange at first because we're not used to it, but we will get used to it; we might even come to quite like it, but we have to do our part to make the whole thing a success."

Philip put his hand up. "Who are they?"

His father rubbed his forehead. "Well," he said slowly, so that it sounded more like "we-ell." "You'll probably recognize some faces from town, and the rest will be tourists, French, American, German...that sort of thing. But the important part is that we make them welcome, that we show them we like having them here, even if we're not quite sure how we feel about it at the moment. Which means that we must always be polite when we speak to them and we mustn't get in their way or make them feel as if they might be intruding. We mustn't go into the house during visiting hours and we can't play in the gardens when the visitors are trying to have a nice quiet time of it."

"But, darling, where exactly are the children expected to play?"

Philip was surprised at this. He hadn't thought that his mother much cared where they played anymore.

Kate said, "I don't really *play*."

"Well, then, where are the children expected to have space to—"

His father interrupted her. "They can go to the lake, the hills, they can play here in the cottage... The visitors will take up a relatively small part of the place, you know."

His mother opened her mouth to say something else but, thinking better of it, closed it again. Philip thought he knew what she was about to say: "Yes, but they're taking up the most important parts..."

Dinner was to end there as Mrs. Connolly had not thought of pudding. Kate got up and again started rifling through the cupboards; this time she found their mother's stash of Cadbury Fingers, high up, where Philip would never have been able to see them. He took two, but no one else seemed to want one now, not even Kate. Before he finished the second biscuit, his mother got up and went into her bedroom. His father wavered a moment before following her. Philip thought worriedly about the blood trail on the file and hoped it was too dark in there for them to notice it.

John

When the day of the opening arrived, John missed breakfast to go up to the house and check that everything was ready. He imagined that Mr. Murphy and his staff must have stayed up very late getting things finished and presentable for the visitors. John had offered to help them, but they had made it quite clear that the arrangement of the furniture would have little to do with how it had been before and that they didn't need his input. It was just as well; he was happy to go to bed. But he had hovered on that precipice between sleeping and waking all night; when he slept he dreamt, and when he was awake, he was conscious of staying extremely still so as not to wake Marianne. Now there was a stinging around his eyes from the lack of sleep that would turn into a headache by the end of the day.

John had paid more attention to the house in the last month than in all the years before the move. He noticed that the intense brightness of the new electric lights, installed at Murphy's behest, changed the character of the rooms entirely. It had the aura, not of a lived-in place, but of a museum whose curators were eager that visitors shouldn't miss a detail. The drawing room was arranged as a picture of genteel hospitality; the threadbare sofas had been replaced with a rather uncomfortable-looking, harder affair, tightly upholstered in royal blue velvet. A book lay open on the table, designed to appear as if someone had just set it down. John ducked under the rope to get a look at what it was: *The Collected Works of W. B. Yeats*. Though he was not a poetry man, he quite liked Yeats and wondered if he might replace this book with another. He thought he'd better not; he imagined that someone had picked it for a very particular set of reasons. The ropes, which bisected the room and indicated where visitors should stand, gave it the appearance of an ocean liner caught in a storm, as if all the furniture had slid to one side. They only added to the feeling that no one had ever really lived there. As he turned to leave, he noticed a pair of velvet slippers by the fireplace and wondered who they were meant to belong to: a fictional him, the real him? John half suspected that the history he'd written had gone straight into the bin and that Murphy had produced a story of a different family, a family more in keeping with the image they wanted to project.

Though the drawing room had been badly altered, the dining room looked better than usual. All the silver, porcelain, and crystal, unused since his wedding day, was laid out, shining, pristine, as if the president herself were coming to dinner. A bowl of very real-looking unreal fruit had been placed on the sideboard. There was less furniture than there had been in his time; it gave the room a more stately appearance.

As John mounted the stairs to inspect the bedrooms, he heard

Mrs. Connolly's voice above the din of young women in the kitchen. He moved through Kate's room first and then Philip's; great care had been taken to make them seem lived-in, despite the ropes. In Kate's, one of those hoops that Victorian children would keep going with a stick was propped against the wall. *How absurd*, he thought—it was a toy for a child from a hundred years ago. In Philip's, his old train set was sitting in the corner, ready to be played with.

In John's own room, the bed had been made up with frilly, expensive sheets and a gold-trimmed bolster. A pair of silk pajamas were laid out on one side and a nightdress, very similar to the one that Marianne really did wear, had been unfurled on the other. Though he knew that it could only be coincidence, especially as every other detail had been quite wrong, John snatched up the pajamas and the nightie, balling them under his arm as he went downstairs.

While the rest of the house was silent, the kitchen was alive. The big table in the middle of the room was covered in trays of scones that had just come out of the oven. An assembly line of three girls was making cucumber sandwiches by the range, a similar line opposite them was making ones with egg. Mrs. Connolly came out of the scullery in her apron, tea towel in hand. She was pulling her fingers away from her palms, as one might open the petals of a flower. It was a characteristic gesture of hers; they were curled stiff with arthritis. John thought that all this must be a welcome change from keeping the house clean and making dinner for the family. He was almost as fond of Mrs. Connolly as he had been of his mother. He watched her now, moving around the kitchen, cajoling the local girls, making sure they were doing things right.

It reminded him of the party he'd had for Marianne a few years after their wedding. He had never organized a party in his life before. At college, it was always Marianne moving through the crowd, talking to everyone, beckoning him from where he stood at the edge of the group, watching. He should have seen it coming, her loneliness. At first, she had thrown herself into life on the estate, bought a set of clothes she thought befitted country life, learnt to drive, shown an interest in the running of the place. But one morning Mrs. Connolly had taken him aside to tell him that Marianne sometimes didn't get out of bed until lunch or, if John was due to be away all day, dinner. It was lonely for her, Mrs. Connolly said; she was used to life in Dublin, he needed to pay more attention to his wife. It was the only rebuke John had ever received from the old woman.

Mrs. Connolly wasn't the first to have pointed out that he lived in his own world. Marianne herself had used different words to say something similar in the early days of their rela-tionship—and to add that he would have to change if they were to remain a couple. He had apologized, he saw her point, but it was only because he and his brother had enjoyed an unusual amount of solitude as children; when he was alone, there had been no one else to think of. Marianne had smiled ruefully and nodded.

But after Mrs. Connolly's warning, he phoned each of their friends to ask them back to Dulough for the first time since the wedding. When he told Marianne, on a Friday morning, that the old crowd would be arriving that afternoon, a slow smile spread across her face and she went to look for her city clothes. They all went swimming that evening, drunk, just as it was getting dark. She found him in the corner of the pool and kissed him. He remembered the others cheering, his own happy embarrassment.

He was filled with shame now, as he stood in the door of the kitchen, that he'd allowed Marianne to become unhappy again.

"Just came up to see how it's going, Mrs. Connolly," he called out.

All activity stopped and the girls, with their healthy, innocent faces, turned towards him. He was struck by the difference between them and the young women he'd seen in Stephen's Green. The housekeeper came over and the girls went back to work, whispering. John was momentarily distracted by how clean Mrs. Connolly seemed, not simply on a superficial level, though she certainly was; but there was a smooth clarity to her skin, her eyes, that seemed to radiate from her insides, like the pictures of the Virgin Mary that hung on the walls of her house. She pinned a stray wisp of hair up as she came towards him; she had no bun or chignon to speak of, but an intricate series of clips kept her scant hair in place. She had worn the same style as long as he'd known her, which was all his life and a good portion of hers. "It's going fine." She pinned the last wisp into place. "Did you get your breakfast?"

"Well, no, but…"

"The girls"—she nodded her head in the vague direction of the cucumber sandwich assembly line—"had a fry-up this morning. There's some bacon left over. It's on a plate in the oven and I'll do you an egg."

John had come to realize years ago that, to Mrs. Connolly, a good meal cured most ills. Even now he remembered the spread she'd put out after his mother's funeral—and probably his father's—although he couldn't quite remember that far back. "You have your hands full. I think I can manage to fry myself an egg."

He saw her consider this for a moment. Usually, she wouldn't even let him pour his own tea. She went over to the range and lifted down a small frying pan. Turning to one of the girls nearest to her, she said, "Put a slab of butter in there, would you, Clare? And give the gentleman help if he needs it."

Clare turned to look at John; she was a lovely girl with fine, honey-colored hair. Her defining feature was a large mole on her left cheek, which was really quite beautiful, he thought. She couldn't have been more than seventeen. John smiled as he walked towards the range. "Thank you, Clare." She cracked the egg into the frying pan. "I don't want to interrupt you, I'll be quite all right."

Once Mrs. Connolly and Clare had gone back to their tasks, John became excruciatingly aware of his body and the space it took up in that kitchen full of young women. As he pushed at the corners of the fried egg with a spatula, he realized that he was going to have to eat in here, that there was nowhere else for him to go. When the egg was done, he slid it onto a paper plate and turned around. Every surface was covered—in scones, butter, jam, teacups, milk jugs, sandwiches, dirty plates and bowls, heaps of tea towels and forks; there was nothing to do but eat standing by the range. He slid a fork out from one of the piles and took a bite. Girls turned around from time to time to get a look at him. When he had finished, he thanked Clare, who was given no time to answer, and was out the door.

Philip

The night before the opening, Philip dreamt, as he had the morning of the move, of Dulough during the ice age, of the valley swathed in snow, of the ice pushing down and gouging out the earth, pulling it towards the sea. There were things stuck in the glacier: boulders, their car, the big house itself. When he looked in the windows, he could see that there were people inside, gazing out at the frozen world.

When he finally woke, the memory of his dream was so real that he felt heavy, as if his limbs, too, were encased in ice. He fought to remember where he was. Opening his eyes, he could see that his mother had left out his good clothes on the chair by the door. She had been in his room while he slept; he didn't like that. He thought of how the men had taken his bed. The visitors were to arrive today, and, though he knew that technically they weren't allowed in the cottage, he was worried that they might come into his new bedroom anyway. When he got up, the air was damp and cold, as if the mist had invaded the house.

On the avenue, big drops slipped from rhododendron leaves into puddles. Philip saw Francis high up in the valley. He hadn't said much about opening Dulough to the visitors, and he was the sole adult who wasn't throwing all his energy into the preparations. His only reaction had been to erect a new deer fence around the house. Philip had seen him talking to the workmen from Dublin one day, showing them how to get a fence post into land that was lined with rock. When Francis turned and walked back off to his shed, one of the men gave him a mock salute. Francis couldn't have seen it, but Philip noticed that he didn't have much to do with them after that.

The front door of the big house stood open and a red ribbon hung in the frame. Philip went to the porch and peered inside. Lights on metal stands blazed into the hall. It was an utterly different place; the chessboard tiles on the floor shone, and shadows—of the sideboard, the hat stand, and the telephone table—fell in new ways. Though every corner of the once dark room had been illuminated, the light somehow made it less real, as if they were in a film. Philip had the sensation of knowing the room well and not knowing it at all.

In the drawing room, thick blue ropes hung from brass stands, which stood in a row, like sentries, down the middle of the carpet. Plastic matting covered the floor on the near side of the ropes, and on the far side, a sofa and chairs that Philip didn't recognize had been arranged into a fireplace scene. A book lay open on a side table. Philip unhooked the ropes and went to get a better look; it was the one with Francis as the fisherman: *The Collected Works of W. B. Yeats*. It was a faded, battered green, with gold lettering. He wished he'd thought to protect it on the day of the move. He scanned the shelves for another that looked like it; the only one he could find was a book about how to identify species of rare trees. Picking up the Yeats and slipping it into his pocket, he put the new one facedown on the table and opened the door as quietly as he could.

He circled up through the house. Every room had a set of blue ropes dividing it in two; he recognized very little of the furniture, which had been arranged to suit a family not his own. To his surprise, his room was the least changed. There was a wardrobe where the wardrobe had been, a bed where the bed had been, even a chair in the corner for an imaginary boy to throw his clothes on before going to sleep. The bed was in significantly better shape than his own; it didn't sag in the middle. He touched the soft counterpane. It must have been brought up from Dublin. A train set, which had been his father's and grandfather's, was set up in one corner of the room. They should have asked him to assemble it; he would have done a much better job.

Without moving the new cushions from the windowsill, he jumped up and looked out over the barn roof. Down below, the hens were clucking in their run like old women. A couple of bikes leant against the hedge, belonging probably to the girls from town, whom he could hear vividly now, below him, in faint murmurs and then loud bursts of laughter. In the distance there was a smattering of snow left on the summit of Mount Errigal, but Muckish and Dooish glowed greenly into the morning.

The white government car drove up to the back of the house and parked on the patch of grass in front of the barn. Mr. Murphy was in the passenger seat. As he opened his door, a second car arrived, sliding into place beside the first. A man Philip recognized from town emerged; it was Frank Foyle, the county councillor. Fat and red-faced, he was always wearing rubber boots with his suit. He went towards Mr. Murphy with his arm outstretched. As they shook hands, the men looked up at the house. Philip stood back quickly and jumped off the sill, leaving the muddy shapes of his feet on the new cushions. He turned them over quickly before running down the back stairs.

In the garden, a marquee was being hoisted into place on the lawn. Men carrying folding chairs and tables flitted in and out of it. None of them seemed interested in Philip, so he walked around, inspecting the preparations. The marquee was really quite big; he wondered how many people it would fit—a couple of hundred, at least? He hadn't thought before about how many would actually come today, but more than a hundred seemed a lot.

He walked around the periphery of the tent, watching how the men battened it down with wooden stakes. It had windows too, of clear plastic, with mock panes. Inside, he could see people setting up. The girls were coming out of the house now, carrying white cloths that they ballooned over the tables. Still more girls came with vases of flowers. They wore what looked like nurses' uniforms—white, with a collar and lots of pockets—but they had tied little black aprons around their waists too. It reminded Philip of the time they'd gone to his uncle's wedding in Dublin; the waitresses serving dinner in the hotel had looked just like that. He wondered if they would be here every day or if this was just for the opening. One of them, a girl with black hair pulled into a neat bun, stopped when she saw him looking in the window. She nudged the one next to her and whispered something in her ear.

By the time the main gates were thrown open to the visitors, Philip was safely back in the cottage. He found Kate in her room. She was sitting on the floor, surrounded by piles of clothes. When he opened the door, she looked up at him despairingly. "I'm supposed to be wearing the dress they got me in Dublin."

"Look at this." He beckoned her out the door, towards their parents' room. The bed was neatly made and the stack of magazines, which had swayed so precariously in the corner since the move, had disappeared, as had the accordion file. He led Kate over to the window. Though it was now late morning, the curtains were still tightly drawn. Where window met wall, he parted the fabric. They peered out.

There were people on the avenue. Having parked their cars down by the gate, they were making their way up to the big house. They were conspicuously tourists, with their brightly colored windbreakers and hiking boots. They took in the steep hills and the dark lake. When they reached the cottages, their eyes traveled first over Francis and Mrs. Connolly's, with its whitewashed walls and red door. Philip and Kate's was another story—the garden remained a sea of mud and the house had yet to be painted out of its gray concrete state. The visitors seemed particularly interested in the new cottage and one couple even stopped at the gate to get a better look.

Philip said, "Do you think they want to come in?"

Kate pulled him away from the window.

Philip wasn't sure what time the opening was to begin, but he knew that they were to wait in the cottage until their father came to bring them up to the big house. It was boring to hang around, and, after he'd had a late bowl of cereal, he fell asleep on top of his duvet. His mother woke him with a warm facecloth. His father and Kate were standing at his bedroom door, watching.

"It's time we went up, darling." With her hand on the small of his back, she passed the cloth over his face.

As they walked across the gravel towards the marquee, the girls were ferrying plates of sandwiches between the house and the tent. They were tiny finger sandwiches, made of fluffy white bread with the crusts cut off. Philip thought he saw cucumber poking out the side. He wanted one of those.

It was evening inside the marquee; the plastic windows didn't let in much light, which made the visitors' faces look greenish. There must have been at least a hundred people, but Philip knew that he wasn't very good at maths, so it was hard to tell. The tables had plenty of sandwiches and scones, and the girls wove amongst them, filling up tea and coffee cups. Local voices were all but lost amongst French, American, and German, but the visitors' voices perceptibly died away when they recognized that the family had arrived.

The tent was much bigger from the outside; when they went in, the family had to squeeze themselves between the visitors to get to the makeshift stage at the far end. His father seemed to know lots of people; he said hello to someone at almost every table they passed. Philip held on tightly to his hand, but his mother and Kate lagged behind, standing over by the door. They had to go back and fetch them, which Philip could tell annoyed his father.

When they reached the stage, Frank Foyle met them, hand outstretched, just as he'd done earlier that morning with Mr. Murphy by the barn. When the farmer-politician reached down to pat Philip on the head, he got a good look at his red nose, the broken veins crisscrossing it like forked lightning. Mr. Foyle put his hand on Kate's head, too. Philip grinned at her, but she was too disgusted to smile back.

Mr. Murphy slowly came forwards from the back of the stage. He was very tall, much taller than Mr. Foyle, and a lick of his hair stood straight up at the front. When he shook hands with Philip's father, Philip saw that they knew each other quite well; his father called him "Michael" and uncharacteristically clapped him on the shoulder. Philip and Kate were to sit between their parents on a row of chairs lined up at the back of the stage, with Mr. Murphy and Frank Foyle at each end. Philip turned to his mother; she was looking straight ahead. It was impossible for him to tell what she thought of all this, but he wished that she would turn to him, even for a second.

The audience watched the stage expectantly, ready for a little entertainment. Frank Foyle blew into the microphone. "Thank you for coming. We'd like to extend a warm welcome to you all, whether you're from across the water or just down the road."

He paused and turned around.

Philip's father put his hand down and gently silenced Philip's feet, which had been thudding against the legs of the chair.

Frank Foyle smiled indulgently and went back to his speech. "Today's a great day, a great day indeed..."

Philip sat directly opposite one of the plastic windows that looked out over the forest. He could see the trunks, dark and wet, and the giant ferns with leaves that cupped water for days after rainfall like they'd had last night. The path up there would be very muddy today, he thought, as Francis stepped out from behind a tree and peered in at him over the heads of the audience. Philip lifted his hand to wave, but the old man turned away and was engulfed by the forest again. Had Francis seen him? He wasn't sure. But there he was again, closer now, not ten feet from the edge of the tent, looking in through the distorted panes. Philip waved and the audience turned to look behind them. Frank Foyle faltered for a moment but kept going, glancing up from time to time to see if they'd come back to him.

"Now, if you'll permit me. I'll let you in on our plans for this grand old place. We have been awarded a very generous grant from the Office of Public Works." He turned and nodded at Mr. Murphy. "And we have ambitious plans, ambitious plans. In addition to opening the house for guided tours, which you'll be able to partake in the enjoyment of today, we'll be building a Visitors' Center down by the front gates, in the field where yous all parked your cars this morning. It will be a state-of-the-art, eco-friendly edifice, built right into the side of the hill so as not to disturb the natural habitat. There'll be a restaurant serving full lunches, museum-type exhibits about the flora and fauna of the area, and"—he paused for effect—"a state-of-the-art cinema, which will show a film about Dulough. In the evenings there will be provision to use the space for visiting musicians and performances."

Frank Foyle had turned around now; he was watching Kate's and Philip's faces with obvious satisfaction. He made a little clapping motion. Philip understood and, looking out over the audience, began to clap. Frank Foyle smiled down at him. He lifted his hands as if to stop thunderous applause. "May I remind you of all the amenities at your disposal today: Tours of the house will begin in half an hour or so—please assemble outside the front door for that. I'll be cutting the ribbon before the first tour…enjoy the grounds, this great lady behind me"—Frank

Foyle gestured to Philip's mother—"has written a guide to the gardens; they're available by the door. The tearooms will be opening on the patio behind the house at about two o'clock, as long as it doesn't rain, but if so, they'll be in the conservatory, also at the back of the house. Lastly, ladies and gents, we'd ask that you don't go down to the beach or attempt to get out to the island. We're not insured for any of you to be eaten by the sharks."

He smirked at his own joke, but Philip noticed that it was the same thing the men had said when he'd come up from building his hut. He wondered if they'd told Mr. Foyle that he'd been in trouble for going out to the island. He watched for a look that said he knew what Philip had been up to, but he didn't even turn around. Instead he added, "And of course, I'd like to introduce you to the owners of the estate, sitting here patiently behind me. They'll be happy to answer any questions you might have this afternoon. Now, please enjoy yourselves and come back soon; don't forget that every time you return, there'll be more amenities to enjoy."

The audience clapped limply, tired of him now. Frank Foyle turned and shook first Mr. Murphy's hand, then Philip's father's and mother's. People rose in relief. The brightly colored windbreakers and hiking boots made for the door. Philip turned to his parents, but his father was talking to Mr. Murphy, and his mother was nowhere to be seen, she having turned and slipped away as soon as the county councillor had finished his speech.

John

John watched Marianne leave, clutching her guide to the gardens and his history of the house. Murphy had kept his word and printed the whole lot; John was suddenly stricken with panic that Marianne might catch him in the lies he'd written. The IRA had never occupied Dulough. That was a story he'd stolen from his Wicklow cousins. John's brother was the only other person capable of pointing out the falsehoods, but he was in Dublin, most likely on the golf course today, and anyway Phil would have endorsed this decision. But John knew that Marianne would be of the opinion that appropriating Irish history to suit his own ends was very cheap indeed. Though she'd never said it, he knew that she found Dulough's past upsetting. The first time she saw the ruins of those cottages, she'd gone quiet and he had wondered whether she was reconsidering her love for him, a man with Philip the First's blood in his veins.

The rain began to fall softly on the marquee, just as it had during their wedding reception. He remembered that day well, how he'd woken in his bed at dawn, the instant knowledge that there could be no going back now. Not that he'd wanted to go back. He was seized that morning by a need to tell Marianne about Dulough, having, he realized, told her almost nothing. He went to her room and saw the white dress hanging on the cupboard door; her expression told him that he shouldn't be there, that he shouldn't see her before the ceremony, that he shouldn't see the dress—and then he'd watched her reject all that. He sat her down on the bed and in the hour before the hair lady came told her all sorts of things, so many things that he'd been a little sheepish later, when he saw her again, about how much he'd packed into that hour. Unlike in the brochure, he told only truths, the surprisingly small amount of information he had about what had gone on in this place in the hundred and fifty years or so before she arrived. What was he doing? Was he trying to impress her? But she'd already said yes, the evidence hanging there on the cupboard door.

It was she who'd insisted on the chapel, despite the fact that it might fall down around their guests' ears. They had to perform the ceremony at ten o'clock in the morning so as to accommodate the tides. He remembered their family and friends trouping over the beach in their finery, heels sinking into the sand, Marianne's veil trailing in the water, so that later it would leave a sticky, salty trail up the aisle.

Francis had worked hard to get the church ready, pulling weeds from between the pews, cleaning the altar of the remnants of birds and small animals. It was a glorious day; but for one quick shower, the sun shone from early in the morning until after eight o'clock that night, when the stragglers came inside to finish the whiskey and the wine. Mostly Trinity people, he remembered. He hadn't seen that lot in years; the problem with living in such an out-of-the-way place was that no one ever visited. At least there'd be more people around now, he thought.

Mrs. Connolly had done all the food for the wedding herself, with no help, despite the fact that Marianne had circled the kitchen in the days preceding their marriage, offering her services. She had been rebuffed, out of kindness, for hadn't the bride better things to be doing than chopping and peeling? Marianne told him that she had not dared to say, well, no, actually she hadn't.

But the day had really come off very well, he thought. The Irish and English guests alike had been charmed by Dulough. In the middle of the afternoon, when the sky suddenly darkened and for half an hour emptied its contents on Donegal, he remembered children running around the house, playing hide-and-seek, and adults milling, glasses in hand, glad to be on a sofa after those wrought-iron chairs. He remembered standing in the bay window with Marianne, watching the men, who seemed to appear from nowhere, in their white jackets, tipping chairs against tables so that they wouldn't hold the rain. That was the moment he had felt married to her, looking out over their gardens, and past them, to the sea. Someone had taken a photograph, one of their college friends, and John had been surprised, on opening the envelope with the Dublin postmark, not that the photo had been taken without his knowledge, but that he and Marianne were standing inches apart, without touching, which is not how he remembered it.

John had thought, as they drove back from Dublin a few weeks ago, after their weekend in the Shelbourne, that things were looking up, that Marianne had got the anger out of her system. He felt sure they had come to an understanding in that hotel room, a room far grander than his old college digs, but enough of a reminder of their student days to invoke a truce.

He knew better than to follow her as she fled the marquee now. Mrs. Connolly was wrong; there had to be unsaid things between husbands and wives, and he had learnt that, though these were the things that saved you, they separated you too.

Philip

A few hours later, the ribbon cut and the tours begun, Philip
was back in the big house. He had come to ask Bríd, the guide,
if he could hear one of her talks. He stood in the hall, listening,
but there was no sound, not even the girls in the kitchen.

He went upstairs, the new carpet as soft as grass. Still nothing.
Instinctively, he turned towards his bedroom; the door was open
and there was a smear of mud on the threshold. He skirted the
room with the intention of going out the other door and disappearing down the back stairs, but at the foot of the bed there
was a little boy playing with the old train set. The boy was holding the pea-green engine and running it roughly backwards and
forwards over a lone piece of track. The rest had been pulled
apart and lay scattered on the floor. A signalman was wedged
underneath the cupboard door, his head cracked and lolling to
one side. As Philip stood, wondering what he should do, the boy
looked up.

Philip strode over to where he was kneeling and grabbed the engine out of his hands. Mr. Murphy had asked if it could be used as a *prop;* he had not said that it would be *played* with. This was not what he had agreed to. The boy fled underneath the bed. Philip bent down. "This is my bedroom." The boy looked out at him from behind the folds of the counterpane. "You've got to be careful; if you run it hard, you'll break the wheels, see?" He turned the engine over and held it up to the boy's nose, so he could see the row of wheels that ran along the bottom. Then, handing the engine back, he pulled the broken signalman from underneath the cupboard door, examined him carefully, and slipped him into his pocket to be glued later.

Sitting cross-legged on the carpet, Philip put a pile of miniature people in the gap between his legs, so that they wouldn't be stepped on. He began to assemble the track. The boy stayed quiet under the bed. Philip had nearly forgotten about him when, after ten minutes or so, he crawled out and sat opposite. Philip handed him a few pieces of track as a peace offering.

When they had finished, it spiraled around a good portion of the room. They began to assemble a long train of cars.

"You just have to push the button there," Philip said. "And it'll go."

The boy pushed the button and the engine started off.

"I'm Philip." The train went through a tunnel. The boy didn't offer his name in return. "Philip," he said again. "This is my room, we're just letting people visit." But the boy was too interested in following the little train's progress to answer. Philip grabbed it up from the tracks and held it to his chest. The wheels spun furiously. "What . . . is . . . your . . . name?" He sounded out each word in case the boy was a foreigner.

"Jamie."

"Jamie," Philip confirmed, handing him back the engine.

They played until they heard the guide's voice coming along the landing. Philip dived under the bed. The bed was very high, and he was able to lean back against the wall. He tried to breathe as quietly as he could. Luckily, Jamie didn't follow him; he was too engrossed in trying to help the tiny passengers board the train.

The door opened and ten pairs of feet came into the room, settling on the plastic sheeting just the other side of the blue ropes. A woman said, "Jamie!" as a set of arms swooped down and picked up the little boy. He began to cry. A male voice apologized and bent down to tidy up the train set. He was rougher with it than Philip's own mother or father would have been. Pressing his back against the wall and pulling his knees up to his chin, Philip hoped that Jamie's father wouldn't stoop low enough to see his hiding place.

There was Bríd's soft voice: "Not to worry, not to worry." But her tone changed when she began her talk. "Ladies and gentlemen, welcome to the final part of our tour. This was originally a servants' room—that door over there leads to the back stairs and down to the kitchen—but was converted into a family bedroom sometime after World War Two..."

Philip could hear the visitors murmuring their interest in his room. He heard a creak as someone opened and closed the cupboard door.

"I'm sorry, sir, but I'm going to have to ask you not to touch the furniture."

"Which of the ones we saw today slept here?" Philip thought it might have been Jamie's father. He hoped Jamie stayed quiet.

"That would have been their youngest, Philip," Bríd answered. "Into everything, so he is, loves getting up to all sorts of mischief."

Some of the visitors chuckled. Philip had only met Bríd once, so he wondered how she knew this. For the second time that afternoon, he felt that people—his parents, Mr. Foyle, the workmen—had been talking about him when he wasn't around. He wondered what else they'd said, and whether Bríd would give away this fact each time she brought a group into his room.

She finished her tour by giving some history of the furniture, telling visitors that it hadn't been moved for more than a hundred years. Philip knew this to be a lie; it had arrived from Dublin over the past few weeks and been made to *look* as if it belonged in the house. He wanted to crawl out from his hiding place to tell them.

"Now, if you'll just follow me. We'll go down the back stairs and into the conservatory, where our tour began. You can find your way out to the gardens from there. Thank you for your attention, ladies and gentlemen. You've been a great group altogether. Please enjoy the rest of your visit and come back soon."

Philip made sure to leave a healthy gap between the group's departure and crawling out from under the bed. After making his way quietly down the back stairs, he slid along the kitchen wall and into the conservatory. There were clusters of white wrought-iron tables and chairs amongst the potted ferns, and a long serving counter against the inner wall. It looked very different to the room that he and Kate used to play in on wet days. He could hear the rain now, dripping onto the glass roof.

He watched the last of Bríd's tour disappear through the outer door, dodging a stream of water as they went. Inside, seated by the window, was a large woman. She wore a pink tracksuit and her tummy bulged out the bottom of her jumper, falling onto her thighs. She sat with her legs apart, planting her runners squarely on the tiled floor as if she was aware that her great body needed firm support. When she sensed Philip looking at her from behind one of the plants, she turned around to face him. She was holding a scone with strawberry jam and cream halfway to her lips, and there was a smudge of icing sugar on her cheek. She smiled at Philip. "You're one of the family, right?" She was American, but her voice had something else, too, as if she might have been born in a country where they didn't speak English.

Philip came out from behind the plant. He was afraid of her in a way he would not have been if she were a normal size.

"Philip, right?" She waved a glossy piece of paper at him. "I've read the brochure. How goes it?"

He stood by her table with his hands in his pockets. "I don't know," he said honestly.

"Why don't you sit down and have something to eat?"

He eyed the plate of cucumber sandwiches; he hadn't managed to find any extra ones after Frank Foyle's speech. Sliding into the chair opposite, he smiled shyly. "Thank you."

She took a bite out of her cream-covered scone and pushed the rest of them towards him. "And these are for you when you're done."

The fat lady didn't seem concerned whether he talked or not. She looked contentedly out the window as he finished two sandwiches. When he reached for a scone, she said, "You want something to drink?" and nodded in the direction of the serving table. He wasn't sure if it was polite to say yes.

"Why don't you get yourself a soda or something?" She handed him a five-pound note. "Will that be enough?"

"Oh," Philip explained, "I don't need to pay. It's my house."

The lady looked at him for a moment, her head cocked to one side, like a parrot's.

"Okay." She put the money back in her handbag.

One of the waitresses was assembling a tea tray for a visitor. Philip ducked behind the serving table and took a paper cup from a stack by a silver machine that said Coca-Cola on it. He eased the plastic lever forwards and let the black liquid fall into the cup.

"Philip!" Mrs. Connolly said from the kitchen.

Coke went all over his shoes and socks. He looked down at his feet and then up at her. She was beside him now, throwing a tea towel on the floor to mop up the mess. "What are you *doing, alannah?*"

"Getting a drink."

"This is a restaurant now—you can't just help yourself. People have to pay here. The money goes to the government, to Mr. Murphy." Her voice trailed off as she got down on her hands and knees to wipe the floor.

Philip knew that the whole room had heard what she'd said. He couldn't look over at the lady who'd given him the sandwiches, though he realized that she must be watching. A wave of anger at Mrs. Connolly rose in him as she swabbed at his feet. He wanted to hurt her while she was down there; he could kick her, he could stand on her hands. Instead, he turned and ran out the conservatory door, shoes sticking to the tiles.

He ran through the kitchen garden, past tourists with umbrellas, doing their best to ignore the downpour. Soon he was out the door in the red-brick wall and into open land. He followed a path overgrown with rhododendrons and passed a sign: PLEASE DO NOT GO BEYOND THIS POINT. The grass was wet and knee-high; the water soaked through his trousers and took the stickiness from his shoes. His face was wet too. Putting his hand to his cheeks, he wiped as roughly as he could. He climbed up the hill, making for the forest. Under the leaves he was protected from the rain. He could slow down now, catch his breath. Sitting on the roots of a big tree, he waited.

When his heart slowed and his breathing returned to its usual pace, he was able to hear the rain dripping through the leaves and the wind rushing around the edge of the forest, trying to find its way in. He walked along the path. The little labels on green spikes had been put back. He wondered how they'd managed to find where he'd stashed them. *Pinus contorta:* lodgepole pine, he said to himself. Did they know it was him who'd pulled them all up? He didn't care now anyway.

A wood pigeon called out eerily from somewhere in the branches above him. He ran on, his feet falling soundlessly on the wood-chip path. He burst out the other side of the forest, where the cliffs fell away to the sea, and the grabbing claws of the peninsulas stretched left and right. It had stopped raining and the sun had come out.

Scrambling down the cliff path, his shoes filling with sand, Philip left the festivities behind him—his mother, father, and Kate, Mrs. Connolly, Mr. Foyle, Mr. Murphy, the visitors, the gardeners with their John Player Blues—and headed for the island.

There were no jellyfish on the beach this time, but last night's weather had washed up great mounds of bladderwrack, black and smelling to high heaven, with little crabs wriggling in it, making busy circles around it. Philip was careful not to step on them; the crunch of shell and gray meat was something to be avoided.

The tide was well in; it ran up the sand and retreated again, like a game. But it advanced a little every time and the little was more than you thought. He checked the headland to make sure he wasn't being watched. Scanning the cliffs like a soldier with binoculars, he could see the top of the marquee, its roof gathering into a point like a big top.

When he got to the water's edge, he took off his shoes. He tied the laces together and slung them over his shoulders. He rolled up his trousers. It wouldn't be enough; he could see that the water was deeper than that around the island.

The sea was cold, of course, bitingly, gaspingly cold. But he was used to it. He moved out, ankle-, then knee-high. Over the rolled-up bottoms of his trousers, to his thighs, his groin, his small hips and protruding tummy button. He kept his arms lifted until the last second, for it was only when the sea reached your chest that the cold fully entered your body. He knew this. But so does anyone who swims in Donegal.

And his shoulders, finally down, underwater, his arms working, breaststroke, pulling forwards, the current underneath, water churned up from the interruption of the island, pulling at his legs, his heart beating fast like in the forest, his breath the loudest thing in his ears, louder than the Atlantic even.

SUMMER

Marianne

At college, I had seen John around for a few years before we started going out together. There were things that made him different: his shirts with their frayed collars, the fact that he sometimes wore a tie, his carefully combed hair. He was always on the edge of everything, peering in, as if the rest of us were exotic fish he longed to swim with. He was otherworldly, if that's not too grand a word.

One evening in third year, we ended up at the same party. It was me who approached him. I knew his name already and he knew mine, but we pretended not to, because to have admitted it would have been to acknowledge how strange it was that we'd never spoken before.

I was going to say we drifted together, but I know now it isn't true. I thought it was a funny coincidence that after the party I started seeing him everywhere. Then I worked out that it was no coincidence; he'd engineered the whole thing. Knowing John as

I do now, I'm still surprised he was so forward; he even turned up in my lectures. Within a few months, we were sharing a bed.

The assurance with which he kissed me and brought me upstairs in his little student flat didn't give away the fact that he was a virgin. It's not as if I really knew what I was doing on that front, either; there'd been a few guys in college, but not enough of them for me to really have any sort of head start. We've never talked about this directly. I've never said that I know I was his first and he's never admitted it to me. Not that it matters much, I suppose.

From our first conversation, I knew he was from Donegal. I'd only been there once, as a child. I remembered a very long rainy holiday, where even my resourceful parents despaired of the weather. We never went back. Instead, our summers were spent in France, camping, the car packed to bursting and loaded onto the ferry.

John was careful in those first months not to tell me the truth about his background. "Dulough" was a word he used often, and even though my brain did an automatic translation from the Irish, I never thought to ask why his house was called "Black Lake." Where he was from was beside the point then. Our world was making toast together in the mornings before one of us ran off to a lecture, meeting in the pub for lunch, sitting side by side in the library, and then my favorite part of the day, cooking dinner in the evenings. I had never thought of myself as having any sort of domestic aspirations, but I loved it.

When John announced that he thought it was time I visit Dulough, I was flattered that he wanted to show me where he was from. By that stage, he'd been to my parents' often for dinner. My mother could see that I was quite serious about him, so she wasn't worried about my disappearing for a week of the Easter holidays up to Donegal with my "young man," as my father called him.

The drive up was great fun, just the two of us in his car, leaving the city, stopping for sandwiches, zipping through all those little towns in the middle of Ireland, where you'd wonder how people didn't die of ennui (that was the sort of word I might have been guilty of using then), and through the border. The soldiers made us completely unpack the car whilst they searched it. When I asked them jokingly how we looked suspicious, one of them fixed me with a stare and insisted it was random. But it upset me, the whole thing. I'd never been through the North before, and I felt exposed, having our possessions removed from John's car and laid out beside it. Not that they'd opened our bags, not that they'd been anything but polite, but it soured the journey for me, and I asked John if he'd ever thought of going around by Sligo to avoid that sort of thing.

"Actually, that's never happened before," he assured me, bemused at my indignation. "They have a pretty awful life," he added.

I felt I was being rebuked for my reaction. I was quiet all the way through Enniskillen and well past the border between Fermanagh and Donegal. For the first time I was rethinking our relationship. I was angry at him for his calm forbearance as the soldiers searched his car, at his diffident smile, at his lack of understanding as to why it had made me feel so strange. My anger grew the further we went. I considered telling him that I'd changed my mind, that he should turn the car around. I wanted to go back to Dublin.

But there's a point, somewhere in Donegal, where you suddenly realize you've left everything behind. You're on a road in the middle of nowhere, turf bogs on either side, and beyond them, the steep sides of a valley. No one dares to build there anymore; only the ruins of Famine houses appear now and again. There are no trees, and the earth has a scorched look to it, as if a fire passed through a long time ago. Later I learnt that the fire was wind.

I still don't know whether it was by design, so eager was he that I see the Poison Glen at its best, that we turned onto that road when dusk was beginning. I simply forgot I was angry with him, the landscape was so beautiful. At the end of the road, a set of gates loomed ahead of us. John got out of the car and dragged them open. I wanted to help, but he waved at me to stay in the car. He was well used to opening them, I could see that. I'd no idea until that moment what he'd come from. I knew there were people like him hidden around the countryside, but I hadn't given them a moment's thought in my life.

I remember my heart convulsing slightly when he turned onto the avenue and drove along by the lake, before bringing the car to a halt in front of the house with as little ceremony as possible. All his actions were muted, as if he was trying to use his body to offset the grandeur of the place itself. He turned to me nervously. "Here we are." Unlike the landscape, the house itself wasn't so much beautiful as it was imposing. I looked from John to the place he'd grown up and tried to reconcile the two. The impression he gave of being a little cut off from everyone else in Dublin made sense now. I could see that he was very different from us, that his experience of Ireland had not been our experience, that we'd grown up in different countries. But of course that realization was subconscious. All I consciously felt was fear.

I was the one in my element in Dublin; without any warning, the tables had been turned.

"Well, come on then," he said, and went around to open the boot. While his back was to the front door of the house, a woman emerged. It was Mrs. Connolly, more robust then, straight backed. The arthritis that took up residence in later years had not yet arrived. She opened the door with such authority that I forgot John's mother had died and assumed it must be her. John turned when he heard the sound of the door opening, dropped our bags on the gravel, and went to greet her. She rebuffed his embrace kindly and instead stood still, holding each of his hands in her own, arms outstretched, so that she could get a good look at him. Then her head popped to one side and found my gaze through the car window.

It was unfortunate, I recognize now, that the first time I met her, I had only just realized what a grand boyfriend I had, because my face must still have registered the shock. John introduced me, not as his girlfriend but as his "friend," Marianne. This startled me anew. It felt like a double rejection; on top of the fact that it was possible I might not be posh enough to have a boyfriend with a house like this, he was suddenly unsure I was his girlfriend. Of course I understood later, as I became more accustomed to his world, that he never would have said "girlfriend" at Dulough, it would have been too forward, would have suggested too much. I wish I'd understood that at the time, though.

As Mrs. Connolly led us into the house, John seemed very concerned for her well-being after his mother's death, much more concerned than for his own. He asked about Francis too, the lovely, quiet man I was yet to meet. It would be years before he and I had a proper conversation.

The hall has never been Dulough's best feature, being dark and, I think, messily designed, with too many doors and corridors sprouting off it, and I hoped that perhaps the house wasn't as grand as all that, that the outside had been misleading. As we ascended the stairs, I looked at the huge tapestry hanging on the wall halfway up. It was a hunting scene, but one in which—and this feeling grew in me the longer I lived at Dulough—I couldn't help but feel that the fox was going to get away as it leapt exuberantly out of the picture, whilst the men lagged behind on their horses, looking slightly lost. In the distance, on a hill, I could just about make out a stag, its antlers outlined against the brown sky (everything in the tapestry had faded to a shade of brown); it too was mocking the hunters.

On the landing, there was an endless set of doors leading to unseen rooms. The scale of Dulough washed over me completely then; the terraced house I'd grown up in could have fitted into this one many times over. Mrs. Connolly showed me first to my room. It didn't come as a surprise that John and I wouldn't be sleeping together, but he looked embarrassed that we were so resolutely being separated. I think now that he was reading too much into it; it would never have occurred to Mrs. Connolly that an unmarried couple would sleep in the same bed.

Anyway, I loved the room she put me in, and after I saw all the others, opening and closing each door secretly over the course of my stay, I came to understand that she'd put me in one of the nicest, one of only two with a view of the gardens, and beyond them the island and the sea. It had a sage-green carpet that had seen better days and lovely rose-gold wallpaper with swirls like the tops of Roman columns repeated again and again. All the furniture was heavy mahogany: the big smooth wardrobe, the bedside table, the writing desk in the bay window. There was a fireplace behind the door, but I could see that there hadn't been a fire in a long time. I couldn't wait to unpack my things and get settled. God, I loved it, I *loved* it straightaway. And I wish I hadn't stifled that, I wish I hadn't been too aware of my own background to show them how I felt. It would have done a lot of good in the moment.

"I'll leave you to get settled," John said, and disappeared with Mrs. Connolly off down the landing.

I went to the window and looked out. Below was not one garden but a series of gardens, each with its own theme. Some were luscious, almost overgrown, others stark, austere, more like the Jardin du Luxembourg than anything else. I still can't take in the fact that at the same time as Philip the First was designing those gardens, he was evicting family after family from their homes on the estate. But of course, I didn't find out about them until much later.

After John and I got married, I ordered a statue of the Buddha from India, not so much out of any beliefs of my own, but because of the exoticism of it, and because by then I had learnt more of the man who had built the house; the Buddha's smiling face seemed the perfect counter to Philip the First's austere Presbyterianism. I'm embarrassed by that now, at the ostentation of shipping the thing from India all the way to Donegal. But in my defense, I knew nothing of the real state of our finances.

I got my first glimpse of Francis as I stood there, the last of the light drifting out to sea, the sun gathering it back in. Francis has always moved more quickly outside. Whether the indoors saps his energy, or whether it's deference to the sudden set of codes

that descend on us in a house like Dulough, I don't know. But I
remember that evening he moved like a young man, lean, quick,
at that point under the trees where day had just turned to night.

I wasn't to meet him on that visit. I was introduced to him
only when John and I were engaged, once Francis knew that I
was to be, in his eyes, mistress of Dulough. I remember being
insulted by this at the time, as if I wasn't worth meeting until he
knew I was a fixture, but now that I know him well, I appreciate
this quality in him, the recognition of permanence. Perhaps it's
because he was brought up here, a place where the landscape is
nothing if not that.

In the evening, we had dinner in the dining room. Without
my knowing, John had insisted that Mrs. Connolly leave the
cold roast chicken and salads on the sideboard, so that he and I
could help ourselves when we were ready. It was all part of his
plan to ease me into life there. He understood that the house was
enough to encounter in one day and that being served dinner by
the housekeeper would have been too much. As I ate the food
Mrs. Connolly had prepared for us, no part of me guessed that
this wasn't the way things always were. I even insisted on washing up, and John, to his great credit, acquiesced, even though
he'd probably never spent any time at that sink in his life. I
should have realized, because he didn't know where anything
went once I'd dried it. I like to think the washing-up was one of
the things I did right that week, that Mrs. Connolly would have
known John only did it under my influence and that I had no
intention of getting too big for my boots just because I was going out with the owner of Dulough.

That night I read very late, the stillness of the house settling
in around me. At one point, I put the book down and listened.

I'd never been completely alone in silence before. I was a little afraid; the only other living being—John—was quite far away; his childhood bedroom was at the other end of the landing. The Connollys had retreated to their cottage, of course, which was something else I hadn't expected. I must have fallen asleep not long after this realization, but when I woke it was pitch-black and John was climbing into bed beside me, his feet frozen after the trip across the landing. He stayed in my bed until dawn.

I was unrealistic about what it would be like to live here. That first visit was all awe, and the second—just after John and I got engaged—was playacting. It was only when I came to live at Dulough after our honeymoon, during our first night together in John's parents' former bedroom, whilst my new husband slept soundly beside me, that I began to consider the enormity of how my life had changed.

He was different when we settled down after the wedding. On my first visits, we had spent all our time together, rambling in the mountains, lolling about in the drawing room. Once we were man and wife, he was up and out before I woke, to where I don't know, but I didn't feel I had a right to say anything. I still thought he was doing me a favor by marrying me and bringing me to this place.

I remember my first phone call home. Only a week had passed and I was already lonely, rattling around the house, and John out with Francis tending to what he'd missed while we were away on our honeymoon. "What's it like living there?" my mum said, and I could still hear the disbelief that I'd married a man from the country.

"It's beautiful."

"And what do you do with yourself all day?"

"Oh, there's lots of work to be done on the estate." I said "estate" deliberately to impress her, to remind her that I had married into something. But it was hard for me to have anything to do with the upkeep of Dulough; that was what Francis and Mrs. Connolly were for, and they had John to oversee them. The truth was that I hadn't known what to do with myself, so I'd spent the mornings of my first week in bed. John came back for lunch and never asked what I'd been doing. I was too embarrassed to tell him.

Afternoons, I drove up and down the avenue. Though I had my learner's permit at seventeen, there hadn't been much reason to drive in the city; the bus was all I'd needed to shuttle me between home and my life in town. But I realized fast that I'd want a car if I was to survive in Donegal. It was safe careering up and down the avenue; there was no one to meet and, as long as I didn't drive into the lake, I'd be grand. John was amused by my practicing and took it as a determination to acquire the necessary skills to live at Dulough—which I suppose it was—and this pleased him.

The party he organized for the whole Dublin crowd a year or so after our wedding was meant to cheer me up. He raided the wine cellar, pulled out bottles that his parents had been saving, for nothing, it turned out. When he'd lined them up in the kitchen, I wiped off the dust and sticky cobwebs with a tea towel.

The sound of the first cars arriving carried for miles: the motor slowing on the main road, turning onto the avenue, the crunch of gravel as our college friends parked and spilled out.

We had great fun showing them to their rooms, taking them down to the beach and out to the island, which some of them had already seen when they came to our wedding. Later, Mrs. Connolly set out pots of tea in the dining room, which John laced with whiskey when she left, enjoying every second of it all. He's more social than he thinks. He, made sure to tell Mrs. Connolly she had the night off, that we'd be fine making our own dinner—didn't we have enough food in the freezer to feed an army? She was skeptical, but he put his arm around her and told her not to worry.

Then it was all of us, frying bacon, sausages, tomatoes, bread, the place filled with smoke. John was careful not to let them into the drawing room, where greasy fingers or a spill would ruin the furniture, so we sat around the kitchen table. Then we did the washing-up and dried the plates in one big assembly line. I already knew that Mrs. Connolly would be beside herself if she had to deal with that mess when she came up in the morning.

Late that night, we went out to the pool, its blackness and the lake's one body of water in the darkness. We stripped off our clothes and left them in piles on the drystone wall. John was the first in, jumping high in the air and swearing genteelly when he hit the freezing water. But it was enough to get the others to follow. Looking back, it's a miracle we didn't land on each other. I remember meeting him by accident in the corner of the pool; he drew me to him, his body beautifully warm.

The next day, but for the few who stayed in bed to nurse hangovers, John took us into the hills. We walked through the gardens first; he named the plants and told us which countries they were from. Worried they would think he was too much the lord of the manor, I watched their faces to see if I could detect judgment, but I couldn't. By that point they wouldn't have shown those sorts of feelings to me; he was my husband now.

We left the garden through a wooden gate, passing foxgloves that were nearly as high as ourselves. "You'll have to check for ticks when we get back," John said, and then he added, "everywhere," and they laughed. There was no discernible path, but suddenly we were out by a lake, at the top of a waterfall, the landscape unraveling below us. John handed out chocolate and leant back against a boulder, face to the sun.

Later that day, my best friend from college, Liesl, and I got some time on our own. It was a rare warm day. I was so relieved our friends had good weather, that we'd been able to spend the weekend outside. Sitting by the fire, cozy, whilst the rain batters off the windowpanes is great for an afternoon, but a whole weekend of it can get depressing, especially if you're not used to it. The others were all back at the house, around the kitchen table, beginning the drinking again, though it was only three o'clock. When they started back up, Liesl had taken my arm and steered me out to the garden—and I steered her down to the beach.

We sat in silence for a while, looking out to sea. There was no wind; the waves were so small they didn't make a sound when they broke on the beach.

"It's gorgeous here," Liesl said.

I nodded slowly. Though the weekend had really lifted my spirits, the depression that had set in in recent months hovered like a shadow behind me. I had even wondered over the course of the weekend whether it might have been better if they hadn't come at all; I suspected I would feel worse afterwards.

"So, how's married life?" Liesl said, nudging me.

Of my friends, I had been the first to get married. In fact, that weekend, we were still the only married couple of the group. Liesl was, by choice, perpetually boyfriendless. This refusal must have made her even more attractive because she'd always had men trailing her. This weekend, she'd brought a guy called Mark who I'd never met before. He was a student at the Royal College of Surgeons. I could see, when Mark shyly told the group what he did, that John was impressed. I had already worked out that, though my husband was convinced Dulough was his fate, he respected people like Mark. John was embarrassed that his standing was inherited; he'd rather have earned it for himself.

"I think my husband quite likes your boyfriend," I said to Liesl by way of evading her question.

"So I noticed." She laughed a full-bodied, mischievous laugh. "Maybe you'll be out of a job soon."

Now it was my turn to laugh. "Maybe."

She looked at me. "You're different," she said.

I wasn't sure whether it was an accusation. I'd been very worried what my friends would think when I married John. They'd all been a little amused by his old-fashioned ways in Dublin, but as soon as they'd seen Dulough at the wedding, I understood that, amongst the girls in particular, there was a certain amount of jealousy at the life I was about to step into. I'd never have to worry about jobs or mortgages or any of the responsibilities they were beginning to face. I was inheriting a ready-made standing in the world, just as John had. Liesl was above that sort of thing, though.

"How do you mean?"

"Well..."

It alarmed me that she was choosing what she said so carefully. I braced myself for criticism.

"I don't know. It's hard to put into words." She hesitated. "You're older."

"Thanks a lot."

"No! No, that's not what I mean. Not looks-wise. You're more stately or something."

"In a bad way?"

She shook her head. "No, it's nice, sort of dignified. You've become more like him."

"You mean 'old-fashioned'?"

"A little, I suppose."

I sighed and leant back on my hands.

She went on. "You're a bit quiet, to be honest." She turned away from me and looked out to the island. "Are you all right?"

Was I all right? At that moment, remembering how easily we used to talk, how, even when I was engaged, she and I would go out on the town, I realized how little I'd actually spoken since I'd got married, how the number of words that came out of my mouth had probably been halved or quartered since I'd moved to Donegal.

"I'm fine. It's just a bit of an adjustment." I forced myself to laugh. It wasn't a very convincing one.

"It was a bit of an adjustment for us too. It's a funny thing when your friend becomes a countess or whatever it is you are."

"John's family isn't titled. You know that; I'm not anything."

"Ah, I know, I'm just teasing you, but it's more or less the same thing, isn't it? I mean, you've got servants, for goodness' sake."

"One servant," I corrected her. "And she's a lot more say in what goes on around here than I do."

"What's it like?"

"What's what like?"

"Living like this."

"It's not all it's cracked up to be, I'll tell you that much."

"But it's gorgeous here."

I nodded.

"And John seems so into you."

"I think he is."

She looked at me quizzically.

"No, no, he is. It's just that he does his own thing a lot of the time and I'm at a bit of a loose end."

She looked concerned now. "Why don't you come down to Dublin once or twice a month for a bit of life? You can stay with me."

It was a good idea, I wanted to, but I couldn't tell her that I'd have to ask John for the money. And though it was long before I had any idea we were in trouble, I couldn't bring myself to ask. It wasn't that he wouldn't have given it to me; he'd just never thought that I might need any for myself. I didn't use money on a daily basis anymore; Mrs. Connolly bought all the food, and when we went into town, John paid for everything. A banknote had barely passed through my hands since we'd got married. It wasn't embarrassment that stopped me from telling Liesl all this, it was that she'd perceive John as some sort of tyrant, trying to make me into an old-fashioned wife, but that wasn't it at all. I should have told her the truth, though, because when I didn't take her up on her offer, I could tell it hurt her, and that it hurt our friendship. She thought I didn't care about her as much as I had when we were in college, she thought that I *had* got above myself. But hindsight's a great thing, isn't it?

*   *   *

The desolation I felt when they, Liesl in particular, left astounded the both of us, and I think it was only getting pregnant with Kate that pulled me out of it completely. It would have been lovely to have a party every year, but when people started having children, it seemed too much to ask them to make the journey. I just hadn't expected to find the isolation so difficult; nothing about the city prepares you for this.

It was Kate who got me into the gardens. When she was little, John gave us a flower bed and we would dig in it for hours, worms turning around our fingers, the soil dark and wet against the back of our hands. When Kate lost interest, the bed became mine and I surprised myself with its success. This gave me something to talk to Francis about. In the early days, he would watch me, smoking one of his cigarettes, but eventually I got up the courage to ask him a question. Of course, he knew everything about the gardens, where each plant was from, whether it demanded light or shade, how much water it could take. He hated the *Rhododendron ponticum,* which runs wild up here; he was the one with the responsibility of cutting it back. The more time I spent in the gardens, the more I came to disagree with his view of the rhododendron. It isn't a surprise that Francis and I had a different view of things; for him the gardens were a job; for me, a hobby.

When Philip was born, I was a different person altogether. I had become accustomed to Dulough; I didn't long to go back to Dublin anymore. In the evenings, we'd sit by the fire, the wind outside, the rain on the windows, the flames smoking when it blew down the chimney. Before the children went to bed, I'd read them stories, and afterwards, when we had the room to ourselves, I'd lie across the couch, my head on John's lap, with Mrs. Connolly and Francis safely down in their cottage.

By the time I met John, his father was already dead, and his mum was dying up here, and putting a brave face on it, so that when Mrs. Connolly phoned to say she was gone, it came as a terrible shock. I offered to come to the funeral, I admit more out of curiosity to see where he was from than anything else. We'd only been together a few months, but it was enough that it would have seemed normal had I tagged along. That evening he said yes, but the following morning he'd changed his mind. I waved him off and went for a walk along the canal. Now I can imagine him and his brother traipsing out to the island, the men carrying the coffin, wary of their footing at the bottom of the rocks, moving slowly lest they drop it. She was buried in the evening, with the light on the water running down the sand, from cliffs to sea. When we buried Philip, it was in the afternoon, during a particularly low spring tide. It's amazing that the sea still dictates so much here.

It's hard to remember what I believed about John's money at the beginning. He always seemed to have enough of it when he was in college, but life wasn't particularly expensive then. As long as we could afford a loaf of bread, a tin of beans, and the odd night in the pub, we could stay alive quite happily. By the time we got married, I naively assumed that because he had this outlandish estate, he must also have a full bank account, a stash of vague, infinite wealth. He didn't seem concerned about a career when we were in college—and this was when people were leaving for London after graduation because they couldn't find jobs in Ireland.

When the children were very small, he took care to hide our

financial troubles from me, but I began to notice the look on his face when the electricity bill had to be paid or when there was some big outlay for the house or the grounds. Planning ahead is not one of John's strengths, though I admit he has many of them, though I admit I loved him so much when I married him that I could see almost no weakness. But he must have known that we would run out of money eventually. I wouldn't have minded going out to work. I would have happily found myself something to do in those early days when I was mooning about the place, useless. In college, I wanted to be a teacher. Perhaps that salary wouldn't have been enough, but it would have been something. John would never countenance such a thing, but if he'd been honest with me, we might have survived. I remember the night, the children in bed, Mrs. Connolly rattling about in the kitchen, when John asked me, out of the blue, "Do you see us living here forever? I mean, do you ever see yourself living anywhere else?"

"Not particularly." I laughed. "I'm used to it now. It's a good place to bring up the children." I turned around, looked at him, and then understood it wasn't a theoretical conversation. "Why?"

Rubbing the bridge of his nose between his thumb and forefinger, he said, "Phil got most of the inheritance in exchange for me getting the house." He sat back against the couch, the air gone out of him.

I didn't realize that he'd talked to Phil the previous week, that they'd already decided Dulough's fate. John's brother had managed to become a solicitor, to steer college in the direction of something lucrative. We visited him and his wife at their house in Foxrock from time to time, a tidy red-brick with a soulless garden, weeded to within an inch of its life. The order of their existence was such a contrast to the inevitable disorder that came with living at Dulough that it was obvious why Phil had wanted no part of the estate. But, as I found out, it didn't mean that Phil wouldn't be devastated if it was sold—that he wouldn't see John as a failure for losing hundreds of years of family history. As unfair as I thought his position was, I couldn't help but agree that something beyond bricks and mortar, gardens, hills, and island would be lost. What would my husband have been without Dulough? He was as much part of the place as if he'd been constructed out of its soil. He thought he could have lived somewhere else, but he couldn't have.

Kate and Philip were much more realistic about the move than I was. When we gathered them into John's study last winter, it was Philip who understood the implications of the new arrangement. Where would it be forbidden for him to go now? He wanted a precise list, and when he realized that his bedroom in the big house would be off-limits but that other children—children he didn't know—would be allowed in, I wondered what sort of damage we might be doing him.

Just before the funeral, Francis showed me the hut that Philip had been building on the island. I was amazed at the work that went into it; the little stones shoved into the cracks so as to keep the wind out, the bracken on the floor, the neat planks lined up across the roof, which he'd even thought to make sure were covered in creosote. The ingenuity of it.

We each had our rituals those late summer evenings after Philip died. I sat in the bay window of the upstairs sitting room, watching over the island until it got dark. Our daughter almost always emerged from somewhere below me—the forest, the avenue, the beach—and wandered about the gardens; sometimes she snapped deadheads or tried a cartwheel, others she sat cross-legged on the grass. I fretted about the damp seeping into her. But I found nothing serious to worry about in her behavior; these were all things she did before. The only difference now was that she was quieter, but wasn't it to be expected?

One July evening, when I went downstairs and plunged outside, she found me. We walked back down the avenue, slapping our arms to keep the midges away. I could sense that she wanted to ask what I'd been doing, but something stopped her. Perhaps she didn't want me to ask her the same question. So we each kept our silence. When we got back, Mrs. Connolly had put leftovers from the visitors' cafeteria on the kitchen table: potato salad, cold chicken, carrot slaw, lasagna, brown bread, scones, puddings. I thought I would have to cook when we moved out of the big house, but, like a schoolgirl, I returned each evening to dinner ready for me. And each evening I pushed the puddings to the back of the fridge for John to devour when he got in. They would have done Kate no good anyway. I remember when I was exactly that age, the new fold of flesh around my middle, the tops of my arms like the beginnings of wings. I wanted to tell her that it wouldn't last long, that it would be gone in a few years, but that would seem an eternity to her. So I hid the puddings and didn't comment on the fact that she wouldn't wear most of her clothes anymore, anything with buttons. I began planning a shopping trip to Dublin.

That night, we saw another of the films John had been renting for us. I have to admit, I was bowled over by the vigilance with which he watched over that stack, always making sure that there were new ones to see. They were films meant to appeal to women: romance, exotic countries, period pieces. I'm not sure what we would have done those nights without them. Reading seemed to take so much more energy than it used to. Though I'd often run my fingers along the bookshelves up at the house, there seemed to be nothing I wanted to open. What did we do in the evenings before? I can barely remember. The children played, I suppose, or finished up abandoned homework, left behind when the sun came out and we ran outside. John was fortunate to have his work, and it was good of him to realize that Kate and I would need something to keep us occupied, too.

We watched *Out of Africa,* and I sat there, trying to remember from the time John and I saw it years ago, whether there was a sex scene that I should be shielding her from. Then I thought that perhaps it didn't matter so much now that she was almost a teenager. When Robert Redford washed Meryl Streep's hair, down by the river, Kate said something very funny: "You couldn't do that here, it'd be bloody freezing." I don't know where she picked up that word.

In the time between tucking Kate in and going to bed myself, I walked up to the house to see why John hadn't come back yet. The staff had left for the day; the only light came from his study. I thought, when I peeped through the door, that he'd be poring over some of the plans for the Visitors' Center or doing something vaguely worthwhile-looking or official. But he had his feet up on his desk and the chair was swinging back on its two legs, the way we always told the children not to. When I walked in, he very nearly fell, and I think it was the embarrassment of it that made him confess his plans for Kate then.

I still didn't accept it. I didn't think she'd be better off in Dublin. This wasn't something we'd ever contemplated before, when there was no money, and having the money now wasn't necessarily a good enough reason. When John came back, I wanted to tell him that we needed to shield her from those girls, the type of daughters his brother would eventually have, the type of girls I had to go to school with, who'd have played tennis and hockey all their lives, who'd have long, lean limbs and no generosity bred into them for girls like Kate. I wanted to say that she would be much better off at the school in town. If we didn't think it was good enough, we could give her extra help in the evenings or spend the money on tutors, and she would be around the girls from here, who would have enough respect for this place to be nice to her. That would "socialize" her, as John put it, quite enough.

But he insisted that I had to see his alma mater before I passed judgment. We went, just me and Kate, on a morning when the fog came down and settled on the mountains and the water in the air curled our hair before we were even out the front door. We hadn't seen my parents since the funeral. When we arrived, they were pale and deferential. My mother drew Kate into a suffocating hug. They put us in the guest room, in the big double bed they bought when I moved to Donegal in the hopes that John and I would stay. We should have come more often. I knew that my mother wanted to ask how we were coping, how we *really* were, so the first night I went to bed at the same time as Kate, though it was only half past nine and my parents were settling down to a few more hours of television.

The next morning, we were on the road in good time for our ten o'clock appointment. Kate was quiet in the passenger seat. It's a quiet I've got used to, with the odd sigh or breath, as if, tantalizingly, she might say something. The books tell me not to ask questions, to let her talk in her own good time, but sometimes it takes all my willpower not to say, "What... What?" I did wonder what she was thinking that morning. Was she hiding her relief at the thought of escaping Dulough, or was she suddenly afraid of going so far away to school? That was how little I understood her then. As I drove, I tried to pinpoint the moment I stopped knowing what she was thinking. I searched for an illustrative event, a day when her behavior suddenly surprised me, but I couldn't think past May; it was as if a fog came down over that part of my mind, as if my memories were like the Donegal mountains—covered. Perhaps it was my brain protecting me; they are, we're always being told, amazing things. I looked over at her, but she was resolutely staring out the window.

The school was a disappointment. To listen to John, you'd think it was a paradise second only to Dulough. It was true that he'd kept the friends he made there, perhaps more so than the ones he'd made in college. It had relocated to the suburbs since he went, though, the precious land in the middle of town making the school enough money to have much bigger grounds on the outskirts of the city. From its reputation, I expected grand buildings, rolling lawns—to be at least a little intimidated. But a roundabout guided the car onto a long and badly maintained tarmac road, to the right of which were several squat, concrete buildings. In the distance I saw portacabins like the makeshift offices used by Mr. Murphy. It was ugly, and I felt hope rise in me that Kate wouldn't like it.

A woman came to meet us at the front door of the main building. She was the head of the French Department. It was clear that this was her calling, that she took a particular pleasure in selling the school. "Welcome, Katherine! You"—she glanced at Kate—"can call me Madame Fitzgerald, and you"—she said to me with a wink—"can call me Vivienne."

Kate listened to Madame Fitzgerald politely on the tour, inclining her head, looking her in the eye. I wondered when we'd managed to teach her such good manners. Then, out of nowhere, this woman said to our daughter, "And am I to understand it that you've recently had a bereavement in the family?"

"My brother drowned in May."

Yes, he drowned in May, fast, in a matter of seconds, barely ten feet from the beach, with Francis running down the headland and wading into the water. Kate could say it aloud, at twelve, and there I was, nearing forty and lost for words.

"*Ne t'inquiète pas, Kate, on s'occupera bien de toi ici.* Do you know what that means? We'll look after you here."

And I was outraged that John had told them, that he'd sent me down unarmed. And worse, Kate.

At the hockey grounds, Madame Fitzgerald nodded to an artificial grass pitch surrounded by floodlights. Girls in short gray skirts, their mouths protruding with gum shields, passed balls back and forth. "That," Madame Fitzgerald said with reverence, "is the first eleven. They're getting a head start." And when Kate and I looked blank, she added, "For the season." Kate studied the girls, with no idea what a first eleven was. None of them looked up or seemed to take any notice of their French mistress leading us around, but there was a self-consciousness to their playing, a tight showiness to their passes that suggested to me that they knew they were part of the advertisement.

The last leg of the tour was the dorms. The girls shared cubicles made for two, a narrow bed on each side, little lockers, a wardrobe, and a chest of drawers. The mattresses were thin, the walls covered in stains left behind by Blu-Tack. I tried to imagine Kate whispering to the girl in the next bed after lights-out.

Outside, I thanked Madame Fitzgerald and told her that we would be able to find our way back to the car park ourselves.

"So, what did you think?" I asked Kate.

"I don't want to play hockey."

"You don't have to, darling," I said, rejoicing.

"I think Madame Fitzgerald said you did. She said everyone plays."

"You could swim. It couldn't possibly be as cold as it is at Dulough." I looked at her and smiled, feeling generous, relieved.

"Yes," she said, tiredly. "I *could* swim, I suppose."

She talked as I drove us into town. She asked what it was like to grow up in Dublin. I told her that it was not as nice as growing up in Donegal. Did she realize what a privileged childhood she'd had—that most children don't live in big houses and ramble infinitely?

For lunch, we went to Grafton Street, to the Bewley's that isn't Bewley's anymore. John and I used to go there when the pubs closed. The first time I brought him, he was taken aback at having late-night breakfasts, having been brought up under a regime of set meals at set times, but I soon got him hooked.

The new owners had kept the old chairs and the stained glass windows, which I was glad of. The menu these days was all panini and pizzas. We each had a caprese panino. I imagined that Italians would be appalled by what passes for their staple in Ireland, watery cheese and a couple of cold, tasteless tomato slices on a baguette. Kate asked to try my coffee. She sipped and made a face. I laughed. She wasn't so grown-up yet.

We shopped at random, wandering in and out of inappropri-
ate places, neither of us knowing where to go. I was struck by
the cheapness of even expensive clothes, by the bad quality of
the fabric, by the shoddy cuts. Kate ran her hands along jeans,
sweatshirts; she avoided dresses and skirts like the plague. It was
a relief to buy her some new clothes; even if I didn't much like
her choices, I was glad she'd be less self-conscious now. In the
changing rooms, we looked at each other in the mirror. I could
be passing my flesh on to her: As my body collapses in on itself,
hers grows.

That night, when Kate was brushing her teeth, my dad called
me into the sitting room. I was worried he was going to ask me
about Philip. Instead he said, "You're in for a bit of weather." I
looked at the forecast; there were big swirls over the Atlantic. To
be honest, I was glad to have an excuse to leave earlier than we
meant to; the sooner I got Kate away from the pull of the city,
the better.

The next day, we did the journey back up in less than four
hours. A record for us. It felt good to see John waiting there
at the window, to know that he'd been looking forward to us
getting back, that he'd felt our absence. I swung the car into
the driveway. Kate got out, gave him a very teenager-y hug, and
went off, lugging her shopping bags into the house. He came
around to my door and spent the rest of the hug that was intended for Kate on me. And out of the blue I was crying, quite
literally, on his shoulder. "Did something happen in Dublin?" I
shook my head like a child, no, nothing in particular. He held
on to me there as I soaked his shirt, so that afterwards he had to
find another one. Now that I knew she didn't want to go to that

school, I found that I was nearly able to forgive him for trying to send her.

When I'd finished, he made me a cup of instant coffee and told me that he and Francis had spent the day looking for the deer herd and battening down the hatches. He'd even taken the Buddha and hidden him in the shed. I began to worry about the new garden, exposed up there on the hill, the rhododendrons not big enough to shield it yet.

As we sat at the kitchen table, Kate came out in a new pair of jeans and a t-shirt, but, God bless him, I don't think John's noticed the changes in her body. She moved noisily about, making herself a cup of tea.

Later on, the wind became a living thing. I could hear it gathering in the hills, rushing towards the cottage, hurling itself at our bedroom window, so that I worried the glass might blow in. It was impossible to sleep. John regretted not staying up at the house, picturing what he might find in the morning. I reminded him that it wasn't the first storm, that we were well prepared. But my imagination wasn't far behind his. Outside, in the darkness, I could picture the trees bending with the wind, plants uprooted and carried away, walls toppled, and fierce waves. I pulled my mind back from the island as best I could, from the blackness that surrounded it, from the gales that blew over it, from the loneliness that enveloped it on a night like that.

We emerged early in the morning, almost sleepless, moments after the Connollys came out into their own front garden. We walked down the avenue, the five of us, and rounded the main gates. The house was untouched. We surveyed it thoroughly—there was not a broken window or a fallen drainpipe, and we could see no evidence of tiles having come off the roof.

Mrs. Connolly went to the kitchen to get a head start on the day's baking and Francis went off in search of the deer. John walked with me through the grounds and up to my garden on the headland. It had been more or less spared too. We stood side by side, looking out at the dark, flat sea, the calm of it making us wonder whether the wind and rain had really ever happened at all. Then we saw the island. The point on the horizon which had been occupied by the church was empty.

We scrambled down to the beach and up the slippery rocks. The church had collapsed in on itself, the walls toppling into the nave, crushing the last of the soft, rotten pews. Even the marble altar was chipped and cracked from the falling debris. John picked his way amongst the mess and ended up squatting next to Philip's grave. I was glad we hadn't chosen the headstone yet; there had been nothing for the storm to damage. I knelt down behind my husband, the wet of the long grass seeping through to my knees, and leant my head against his back.

Further up the coast, the sea had climbed over the public beach and washed through a row of cottages, taking chairs and tables and beds with it. Fortunately, the inhabitants had known what was coming and had left in time. In the days that followed, the water disgorged some of their possessions and they lay along the beach, wrapped in seaweed. The former owners didn't go down and clear up their furniture. It surprised me that they could stand to look out their windows each day and watch as their things rotted away. Mrs. Connolly told us that the priest had organized a bus for them to go over to the Ikea in Scotland.

I knew without asking John that the church would be left as it was; if the visitors weren't allowed out there, the state would have no inclination to rebuild. After the initial shock of it, John was happy that a monument to the first Philip was gone. I was relieved for a different reason: I'd been dreading the day that one of the tourists would break the rules and explore the island. Now they were much more likely to leave it alone.

The next week, Kate came to my garden. I watched her emerge from the trees and trek up the slippery path. It was the first time she'd taken any interest in it, and I have to admit that I enjoyed showing her what I'd planted and telling her how it would be when it was properly finished. "You used to like gardening, darling. Do you remember—when you were little? You tried to grow sunflowers."

She nodded and twirled one of her boots in the muck. And the knowledge was with me suddenly, coupled with the satisfaction of realizing that I did (at least this time) still know what she was thinking.

"So you're going to go to that school."

"Dad said I should tell you myself."

I nodded and went back to my digging. The satisfaction I got from reading her, and from realizing that it was John who'd convinced her, went away, and there I was, mud up to my ankles, my daughter standing in front of me, decently waiting for me to respond so that she could make me feel better. I bent down to pull away the roots of some tangled weeds and flung them to one side. Watching the toe of her boot twirl in the bed, I sensed her weight shift from one leg to the other. When it became clear that I wasn't going to speak, the boots sucked themselves up out of the ground and walked away down the hill and into the trees.

Before she had fully disappeared into the forest, I followed her, sliding on the steep path, falling on my behind more than once, the damp seeping into the backs of my thighs, the slather of mud across my trousers. I shouted to her disappearing back and I saw her duck down, commando-like, in the undergrowth. What was there to do but walk past, not seeing her, calling her name in the opposite direction, and pretend to give up, as I watched her crawl out and run down the path, to safety, away from her mother?

She stayed away from me completely after that, passing the weeks before she went to school in the kitchen amongst the girls from town, whose younger brothers and sisters she would have been in class with, with whom, judging from the laughter I heard as I tiptoed about the house, she would have got on very well.

She went for long walks on her own (she takes after her father). Once, she came back wet to the thigh from where she'd stepped in a bog hole. Another time, after getting soaked by the rain, she stayed out and came back hours later, an awful cold already in her lungs. I was happy when she had to stay in bed. My poor, captive child.

But the moment her temperature dropped, she was up and out and gone for a whole afternoon. When she got in, looking pale and sick again, I read her the riot act and we were back to square one. We were no longer friends, but I desperately wanted to ask whether she felt what I was feeling. Oh, I know that mothers love especially, but how do twelve-year-old sisters love, and do they feel their own form of despair?

She phoned the evening John left her at the school. She said that everything was *fine. Fine,* a word he probably told her to use, a word meant to put her mother's mind at rest. He was right to tell me to stay at home; there would have been a scene. I waited in the cottage, poking at the fire, eating over the sink, drawing the curtains against the darkness. When I look in the mirror these days, I don't think it would be unfair to call myself gaunt, my neck becoming thin and stringy before its time, my hips protruding, sharp, like the shoulders of a bat. My tummy the same, a fold of flesh that arrived with the children.

I lay on the couch and thought about putting on a video. John had been considerate in his choices, avoiding anything that smacked of death. I wondered whether he would watch them with me now that Kate was gone.

The school told us that she was only allowed phone calls home at weekends. There was no time on a weekday, what with classes and games and dinner and prep. Besides, they found that students settled in better if they weren't talking to their parents every night. It stopped them from *bonding* (not my word) with their peers. I imagined the French teacher as being responsible for all this, the inventor of all these rules.

The next morning, I sealed up a letter to Kate, full of easy harmless chatter, and drove straight into town, despite the fact that it was early and that I'd hours until the post went.

Then I slipped into John's study. It was a Monday, the only day that Dulough was closed to visitors, so I had the place to myself. I realize now that what I was looking for was another secret. I hadn't known that John was plotting to send Kate away to school, and I wanted to find out if he was hiding anything else, another horrible surprise that this time I might be able to prepare myself for.

The painting of Philip the First looked as if it was about to fall off the wall. Before I righted it, I stared at him, and for the first time saw a resemblance to my husband. It wasn't in the nose or in the chin, or in any of the usual features that connote family resemblance. It was something else: I saw ownership, not just of land but of history, a firm ownership of their own history.

Straightening the painting, I found the safe behind. I tried the year Dulough was built, then Kate's, then Philip's, birthday. It swung open. Did he change that since? I wondered. Or had he been John's favorite and I'd never realized? First I looked for correspondence from the school, but it was obvious there was nothing from them; everything they sent was stiff, glossy, nestled into expensive-looking folders. Instead, the safe was full of little jewel-colored notebooks, stacks and stacks of what I soon discovered to be Olivia Campbell's diaries.

The oldest diary began in the mid-eighteen hundreds, while she and the first Philip were staying at Lough Power, still a guesthouse then. Her husband is scouting about for cheap land to buy, and Olivia is dismayed at the prospect of leaving Edinburgh, where she has just learnt to live. She has only recently stopped pining for England, for her family home in London, for summers on the south coast. And now Philip wants to come here. But it was not the age of women defying their husbands, especially not husbands like hers.

That afternoon, Kate's first day of school, I flipped through weeks and then years of Olivia's life. Her fear at being trapped here: "I look into the distance and see nothing man-made, nothing to break the endless fields but mountains and more mountains." Then the acceptance, and finally, once the house was built and the gardens laid out, a love of the place that rivals even John's. After five years at Dulough she "cannot imagine living anywhere else," and, when she visits her family on holiday, "Cornwall has been usurped in my heart by Donegal. Nothing can compare to a day here, when it has recently rained, when the clouds scud away over the sea, when the sky is silvery and the sun comes out. I go walking through the glen, the air so fresh, the only sound the waterfall in the distance. To come back to one's own warm drawing room, to a pot of tea, and the knowledge that one will sleep soundly that night, this has become the closest thing to heaven on earth for me."

One of the diaries had a piece of newspaper sticking out of it, which someone had been using as a bookmark. I began to read from there, curious why the reader before me had chosen to signal this particular page of Olivia's writings as significant.

Towards the end of the nineteenth century, she began to worry who would inherit Dulough. Her son, Duncan, wasn't showing much interest in the estate; he had his law practice in Edinburgh, a house in the New Town. He wouldn't come to Donegal unless his mother made him. In 1885, Olivia invited her extended family for a weeklong visit, but it was really a grand interview. They all came, except for a nephew who worked for the British government in Ceylon. Olivia's guests didn't know that such a large inheritance was at stake when they dutifully took trains and boats and ponies and traps all the way from their corners of England to the far northwest of Ireland. They turned up pale and exhausted, horrified at the length of a journey to a country that on the maps had seemed so close.

In the preceding month, Olivia had hired, and trained herself, a dozen or so young locals to act as footmen. Her English guests were met by these Irish boys, who swung the cases and trunks off the back of carriages in wide arcs, no bother to them after the weight of the turf they were forced to lug on a daily basis. They showed the guests to their rooms and announced in tones they hoped were posh enough, intelligible enough to English people, that they were very welcome to Ireland.

As many activities as possible had been planned to keep her guests occupied that week. There were shooting parties for the men and there was tennis for the women. They had picnics in the little glass summerhouse at the top of the cliffs, which was gone well before my time. And there was the option of swimming in the sea, although Olivia notes that no one was brave enough for the North Atlantic, being used to places like Cornwall, which was practically France, after all. Perhaps that, too, was one of her tests. She knew that one has to be hardy to survive up here. But then again, I wouldn't have called myself hardy when I arrived; I'd have picked another word, naive perhaps, idealistic certainly. Are they the same thing? But I suppose hardiness can be learnt.

On the last night, Olivia had a party. She invited her closest friends—the Turner-Adamses, the Williamses, the Whitneys, and her nearest neighbor, Geoffrey Roe—to meet her family, and to help her judge who best to leave the estate to. She also invited her late husband's cousin, Dulough's architect, Charles Wrenn-Harris, telling him firmly that it was about time he saw his handiwork.

Olivia stood outside the dining room as they went in to dinner. Geoffrey Roe hung back. He had soft hair, the color of marmalade, which she suspected he cut himself, and pale, pale freckled skin. He looked like the descendant of Vikings, but he'd not one ounce of Norse blood in him, he said regretfully.

"Mr. Roe."

"Olivia . . ."—he stood back, taking her in—". . . very pretty."

It was the first time he'd called her by her Christian name.

Very pretty, words for a girl, but she'd accept them. She had been old with her husband, and these days she did almost feel as if she were getting younger.

A year earlier, Olivia had received a letter from Geoffrey Roe. He had heard about her magnificent gardens and wondered if it would be presumptuous to ask if he might come and paint them one day. He arrived the following week, carrying an easel and a paint box. His only request was an empty jam jar, which she watched him fill from the fountain and place unsteadily on the grass beside him. It flushed rhododendron pink, sea blue, leaf green. When he was finished, he knocked on the kitchen door and asked if he might have some gin. And a little tonic, if it wasn't too much trouble.

Though she had not invited him, he turned up weekly that summer, always unannounced, always in the same outfit, the jam jar retrieved from a recess in the garden wall. Sometimes she watched him as he painted, from the bay window in the upstairs drawing room. On his fourth or fifth visit, she met him at the back door, gin for both of them, and invited him inside. But it was a lovely evening, he said, why not sit in the summerhouse? In the outdoor room, the glass doors flung open to the sunset, their knees covered in blankets, he told her that these midges were nothing compared to the mosquitoes of his travels, which had eaten him alive, which had given him the taste for gin, the need for quinine.

His weekly visits stopped as soon as winter came, though the estate was beautiful in the snow, though she would not have minded at all if he had painted from one of the upstairs windows. She wanted to tell him this, but couldn't quite work out how—a letter, a visit, a message brought by one of her servants?

And then she overheard one day in April that he was back at Lough Power. "Back?" she couldn't help but ask. Mr. Roe had spent the winter in London. And why should he have thought of telling her? Still, when he arrived the following week, when he retrieved the jar from the wall, when the water ran out because it had frozen again and again, the ice having cracked the glass, she let the housekeeper find him another one, as she hid in the scullery, listening.

But the next time he turned up, she hadn't had anyone but the servants to talk to for weeks. She couldn't help but venture out onto the avenue and invite him inside for something to eat when he had finished painting.

As I read, it became clear to me that when Olivia dressed on the evening of her party, choosing her gown carefully, taking longer than usual over her hair, the knowledge that Geoffrey Roe was coming had preoccupied her almost as much as the house's future. He put his hand on her back as they went in to dinner, and she worried briefly that her family would see, that they would guess—but what of it, she thought, what of it?

After the party, Geoffrey Roe became a daily visitor to Dulough. One afternoon, as the days were getting short, he demanded to be taken out to the island. He leapt over the rocks at its base as if he were a man in his twenties rather than, she guessed, his sixties, a decade she had just entered herself. When she caught up, he was in the churchyard, looking at her husband's grave.

"That space under his name is for yours, I take it."

She had been standing precisely there as he was buried. When the ground was consecrated, Philip had imagined a

Campbell dynasty, the graveyard filling up with his descendants, but she intended to leave Dulough to her sister's son, not their own. Her husband would have been disappointed in her decision—and in their son for his lack of interest in the estate—but what she cared about now was that someone would love Dulough as much as she did. Besides, there would still be plenty of money for Duncan to inherit.

As they came back over the rocks, Geoffrey fell, his right leg disappearing into a hole, his body twirling backwards. He pulled himself slowly up on his elbows and looked down at his foot, which was trapped. First he pulled gently, then hard, holding his thigh with both hands, as if trying to free himself from the jaws of an animal.

Olivia watched. To have offered help or advice to her husband in such a situation would have ensured his fury.

"Well, come on," said Geoffrey Roe. "Give me a hand, won't you?"

"Shouldn't I get Thom?"

"And risk the tide coming in? It would be over my head. Your gardener wouldn't do me much good then, would he?"

She bent down to examine his foot. It was wedged between two rocks at a strange angle. He craned his neck to look at what she was doing. Her hands encircled his calf and pulled up, hard. Geoffrey let out a loud breath, but that was it, as if he had broken all manner of things in the past and knew that this was necessary. Not for the first time, she wondered what his life had been before this.

He would be off his feet for a good while, the doctor said. Olivia's maid, Áine, confided in her mistress that there were no servants at Lough Power, only a washerwoman who came once a month. Who cooked for him? No one, he "cooked" for him-self. Olivia was incredulous. It was clear that he couldn't return to Lough Power on his own, so she put him in the bedroom with the best view of the island, the bedroom in which I'd spent my first visit to Dulough, to remind him that those rocks should never be scaled recklessly.

Though he was well enough by the week before Christmas to return to his own home, Olivia persuaded him that the house would be too cold and that he should remain at Dulough into the new year. Secretly, she had sent Thom to assess the state of his house. He returned with stories of paper peeling off walls and of mice in the kitchen. She wasn't surprised; the land be-gan the process of reclamation quickly. She had learnt this when Philip's tenants were evicted; one of the cottages, which had belonged to a family of women, disintegrated quickly, grass growing in the thatch, the garden going to seed, until the roof collapsed less than a year after the family left.

Thom brought Geoffrey's post when he returned from Lough Power. Olivia presented it to him in the drawing room that evening. As he opened letter after letter, flinging them aside, signaling his lack of interest in their contents, which were, he indicated, about the business of selling his paintings, she told him of the women who had lived in that cottage and how her husband's cruelty was tormenting her now, despite the fact that it was a long time since the evictions.

Without looking up, he said, "When the people here were very hungry, the men often went without—or ate only the skins of the potatoes—so as to feed their families. No one told them that the skins were poisonous. That's probably why there were no men in that house."

Olivia pointed out that she had often eaten the skin of a new potato.

"Well," Geoffrey said, glancing up at her, "if you ate almost nothing but them for months on end, you would die, too."

He had almost got to the end of the pile when one letter made him stop. He read it intently and read it again. It was written on blue vellum, the handwriting unmistakably a woman's. When Geoffrey had bought Lough Power, not long after Olivia and Philip stayed there as a boardinghouse, her husband didn't hide his disapproval of Geoffrey's reputation. He wouldn't tell her why he held this artist in such low esteem, but once, when a guest of theirs mentioned he was to stay with Geoffrey after his time at Dulough, Philip suggested he leave then and there. Snippets of gossip had reached Olivia over the years; Geoffrey had been married once but was reported to have had children with women other than his wife. She never asked him about any of this. After all, what right had she? She wondered now if that letter was from a woman who had a claim over him. She was consumed with fear that he might have to leave.

Geoffrey got up to pour himself a drink when the dinner gong rang. Without a word, he picked up the letter and put it in his pocket. As they walked across the hall, Olivia saw that he had filled his glass to the brim, as if gin were water.

When I looked properly at the piece of newspaper article that had been sticking out of the diary, I saw that it was from the year John held the party for me, not long after we were married. At first I was touched that he had looked to Olivia for advice on how to entertain at Dulough, but the more I read of her writing, the angrier I became that he'd kept her diaries to himself. Why hadn't he given me access to them when they could have done me so much good, when they could have taught me that one gets used to the remoteness, when they could have taught me about Dulough's history, so that I could have felt it was as much my home, too?

I got up off the floor, my knees aching. Picking up the little stack of diaries I'd accumulated, I put them back in the safe. I wouldn't have seen the key hanging just inside the door had the back of my hand not grazed the hook.

I knew, just as I had known that Kate had decided to go to school, the knowledge settling on me easily, unequivocally, that it was the key to the third floor, to what had been intended as Dulough's ballroom. No other door in the house was locked. John had told me—and the children—that the key was lost, that no one had been up there since the house was built.

If I was going to try to get in, I had to do it then. In a few hours it would be dark; in the morning, the tours would start again—and then John would be home. He was staying with Phil in Foxrock until the end of the week. He said that it was to get his brother "up to speed" on estate business, but he probably wanted to get away from me. I don't think I'd said five words to him since Kate told me she was going to that school.

On the landing, I realized I was alone in the house for the first time since I'd arrived at Dulough: no husband, no children, no Mrs. Connolly. I thought about Olivia's maid, Áine, whose mother had lost seven of her twelve children by the time Áine came to work here. Was that worse than losing one? Or two? Because hadn't I lost Kate as well? It settled on me that at the beginning of the summer I'd had two children and that now I had none.

*   *   *

My friend Liesl had a baby a couple of years ago. I couldn't phone her to tell her about Philip; I couldn't phone anyone. John did what needed to be done on that front; he was even the one to tell my parents, which was wrong of me. Liesl saw the announcement in the newspaper and wrote a very kind letter, but I wasn't able to cope with sympathy at all afterwards. I still can't. Especially face-to-face. There's something awful about looking into someone else's eyes and seeing the terrible thing that's happened to you reflected back—or the fear that it could happen to them—or the gratefulness that it didn't. Mrs. Baskin, the chemist, stopped me and John a month or so after Philip died. She was crying. At first I assumed something had happened to her, but then I understood that she was crying for us. I wanted to slap her. I could see that John was embarrassed by how curt I was, but he couldn't chastise me then.

In many ways, Francis has been the best of everyone. He'd be surprised to hear that, no doubt, but just afterwards the only thing keeping me sane was him, beside me in my little garden, helping me get something into the ground, or doing the heavy work I couldn't do. I could have asked some of the new groundsmen; they're all perfectly nice, but I don't want them to think they should be including my garden in their day-to-day business. Francis never comes up without being asked. He talks so little, and when he does it's only about the plants. This is the greatest kindness anyone has done me in the past few months.

I haven't thought much about how he must have felt. Francis didn't tell us that he was watching Philip from the headland when he drowned. It was in the statement he gave to the police. I do remember him playing watchdog that day, prowling around the grounds, irritating John, who thought it gave a bad impression to the tourists. Of course it wouldn't have been Francis's place to criticize the new arrangements, but it was easy to see that he thought it wasn't a good idea, this opening up of the demesne to visitors. He wouldn't have known, of course, that we'd run out of money to pay him and Mrs. Connolly, but I still think that if we'd explained it, they would have wanted to stay; they're both eligible for a government pension now. John thinks that he's the only one with allegiances to Dulough, that the Connollys would leave if they weren't paid. But he's selling them short; once you've lived at Dulough, it's impossible to imagine living anywhere else.

Mrs. Connolly told us that she'd chastised Philip for taking some Coke from the restaurant before he'd run away. But I've never blamed her; I had an inkling what he was up to the day I caught him coming up from the beach, claiming he'd been digging for lugworms, with no bucket, with no evidence whatsoever of that. I knew he was up to something, and I should have tried harder to find out what it was.

It doesn't say in the statement at what point Francis realized that Philip was going to try to swim out to the island, it just says, "I went down to the beach," but he would have torn off like a hare when he understood what was happening. He wouldn't have had a chance of reaching Philip in time, though; it's a long old way down from the top of the cliffs.

I was standing on the avenue in front of the house, talking to a French tourist. And I saw her eyes flick up over my shoulder. I remember thinking how rude she was, that she'd asked me some question or other about the gardens and now she wasn't bothering to hide that she was bored. But the way she looked past me must have made me turn. There was Francis walking towards us with something in his arms. I didn't realize it was Philip straightaway, but then I saw that Francis was wet, and that the thing in his arms was wet. I suppose people would have crowded around, but I don't remember. I only have pieces of that day now, there's no cartilage there, nothing joining the events in my mind. If I looked closely I know I'd be able to see them, but I turn my thoughts away, to getting the gardens ready for winter, to whether I might go and stay with Liesl for a while, to how Kate's getting on at her new school.

The door to the third floor wasn't difficult to open. On the other side was a rough wooden staircase, waiting to be polished and carpeted as befitted the approach to a ballroom.

The ballroom ran the length and width of the house; from the top of the stairs, I could barely see the far end, where a set of three rectangular windows with curved tops looked out over the front gardens. On the gable walls, identical black granite fireplaces faced each other like sentries. The walls were unpainted, the floors unfinished, but it was more complete than John had admitted. To have lived below this for so long, and not to have sensed, somehow, the vastness of the space above us, seemed impossible to me.

By the time the light began to fade, I had all I'd need. The last thing I did was return to John's study and take the diaries, years upon years of them. When I was finished, it was completely dark, not only in the ballroom but in the rest of the house as well. I dared not turn on the lights in case the Connollys saw. Creeping about with a candle, it wasn't lost on me that I may as well have gone back in time, Olivia's writings disturbed, the ballroom opened up again.

Instead of returning to the cottage, I wandered through the house, prodding the burnt patch in front of Philip's fireplace, shoving my fingers into a hole in the dining room wall, looking for other such marks, trying to attach them to events; a careless housemaid (a near catastrophe), the corner of the table catching as those boys moved it out of the way for Olivia's dance. It is not difficult to think of the house as a consciousness, a repository of events, its breath whistling through the walls, our lives playing over and over again in its memory. This is as close as I get to ghosts.

I got to the ballroom early the next morning, before Mrs. Connolly arrived in the kitchen. I had meant to clean. Instead, I took my coffee and sat on the floor in front of the big windows. I could see from the gardens all the way to the horizon. The sea was calm, the sun catching the island. Below me, one of the groundsmen was raking the gravel, something we'd never thought to do in our time, but the minibuses wreak havoc on it when they turn to go back down to the car park, a smattering of tourists inside. There wasn't a weed to be found in the gardens, and the lawn remained perpetually—although I never saw them cutting it—at two inches. Dulough had become foreign to me: the perfect grass, the dustless rooms, the lights so bright that there could have been no illusion whatsoever of a home.

When Philip the First told Olivia of his plans for the ballroom, she was astonished. His religion frowned on dancing, even forbade it. But this was when she learnt about his pride. It was not simply the land with which he wanted to impress their · guests but the house, too. Philip's architect, Charles Wrenn-Harris, had convinced her husband that no house could be

considered grand without a ballroom. And so he had acquiesced, as long as it was situated on the third floor, as long as it
looked like an afterthought, which in many ways it was.

Or he had acquiesced until he saw it, until he walked up
the rough, unfinished stairs and entered the huge room, with
Olivia behind him, her heart leaping for joy. Two grand marble
fireplaces would blaze the damp and cold out before the guests
arrived, and . . .

"No" was all he said before striding out. She followed him,
not wanting to ask what he meant, but knowing all the same.
The next day, the carpenters were summoned. She came upon
them early, on her way down to breakfast. The door to the ballroom was open and they had begun to dismantle the stairs. She
hurried past, not wanting them to see her cry. By the time breakfast was finished, the stairs were gone completely; the threshold
of the ballroom hung in midair above her, unreachable without
a ladder. Later that day her husband locked the door and put the
key in the safe. She had her revenge, though: The same carpenters were summoned to put the stairs back again when he died,
but she was too decorous to hold a ball during her mourning
period—and when Geoffrey Roe came along, her interest in so-
ciety evaporated.

When my coffee was gone, I began to clean. There were ripples
of dust on the floor like the ripples left on the beach when the
tide goes out. It would have been much quicker if I'd had the
Hoover, but I couldn't risk that sort of noise. I swept the whole
space, stopping when I heard the murmur of voices downstairs,
the first tour group of the day. They were beginning to get
smaller, the summer over. Some days no one signed up and I

saw Bríd in the conservatory, chatting to Mrs. Connolly over a cup of tea. If I were Bríd I would have been embarrassed to see me, knowing that she guided people around my old home. But she didn't seem embarrassed—a little shy, perhaps, but not embarrassed. Was it because Dulough looked so like a museum that she couldn't imagine we'd ever really lived here? Or because she thought we should never have been living here in the first place?

I marveled again at our son, at how he realized long before I did the effect the move would have on him. My husband cleverly managed to keep his study. None of the rest of us had the luxury of a room to ourselves. I deserved the ballroom.

When I'd finished, there was no dust left. I had even wiped the fireplaces with a wet cloth. The marble could have been assembled yesterday—its corners were so sharp, its grain so shiny. I ran my finger along the mantelpiece; I needed to find things to put up there, to make the place more welcoming. Some things from Kate's room, perhaps.

I blew up the mattress, the one John and I used on our honeymoon in Italy, when we camped north of Rome. I thought it was because he found camping romantic—and it was—but I realized later that there was probably no money for a hotel. I covered the mattress with layer upon layer of blankets; I remembered how uncomfortable it was, not that I'd cared on our honeymoon. Then I put two upturned cardboard boxes on each side of the bed and covered them with tea towels. At the foot, the chest from Philip's old room, the one he used to keep his toys in. I'd found it the previous night, cast out by the government men who'd obviously thought it too shabby to have in the house anymore. All I needed was a desk. I went down the stairs and listened at the door to the landing.

I took a writing desk and its little chair from a bedroom that hadn't been used since we had all our friends to stay, a back bedroom with nothing to distinguish it except that it was Philip's favorite hiding place. He fitted inside the corner of the wardrobe completely, so that even when we opened the door, he could squash himself into one end without being seen. The first time he did it, we looked for him for fifteen or twenty minutes. It seemed a very long time and I tried to hide my panic. After he died, a part of me believed Philip was hiding in that wardrobe. I still can't shake the notion that he's playing a long game of hide-and-seek, that he's hiding somewhere new, and all we have to do is find him.

I hadn't much trouble with the desk; it was small, a Victorian lady's travel desk with folding legs. I carried it under one arm up the stairs, and then I went back for the chair.

When I got to the top I put them down next to the big windows and began a letter to him, my husband, who has never understood anything.

I leave the following Monday morning. Kate has only been at school a week. John has only been home a few days, his efforts to avoid me almost comical. I get into the car before six o'clock in the morning, in the knickers I've slept in, my teeth unbrushed, my hair wanting a comb. I roar down the avenue, knowing that the minibuses won't be there for hours. There's a tractor out on the main road. I could kill him he's going so slowly. When he turns into a field, I put my foot down for the Donegal bypass and the road to Dublin.

As I drive, the last scene I read in Olivia's diary plays in my mind: She's in the bath, wondering still whether Geoffrey's going to leave, whether she should ask him outright. There's a knock at the door, Áine with more water. But it's him. He doesn't ask if he can come in and he doesn't look at her until he's sitting on the three-legged stool near the taps, the one we still have in there now. He takes out his sketch pad and rests it on his crossed knees. He has a white tin cup with him and she realizes with relief that it is not a drink; it's full of charcoal. His fingers are stained, he has been drawing elsewhere in the house. Olivia wonders what made him stop and come to find her, how he knew she was here. She is aware of her breasts breaking the surface of the water and she wonders whether her hair, gray now and slick against her head, is unattractive to him. She lifts a hand to fix it. *Don't move,* he says quietly. So she closes her eyes and keeps her body still, listening to the scratch of charcoal on paper.

I stop in Enniskillen, at the playground that is the almost precise midpoint in the journey between our part of Donegal and Dublin. Last summer, Philip left his shoes behind in the car park. He took them off before settling in for the rest of the drive home and forgot to pull them back inside. I blamed Kate for distracting him, but it was my fault for not checking.

The school is more cheerful than I remember; there are lots of students around now, huddled in groups, moving between buildings, running up the path that leads to the sports fields. I have Kate's timetable in the glove compartment. Elevenish on a Monday, the beginning of her history lesson. It's easy to find the classroom. There are only three buildings and each is clearly labeled. Putting my hand to my hair, I wish I'd thought to look in the mirror before getting out of the car. I peer through the thick, institutional glass in the door and knock. The teacher turns from the board, surprised.

"I'm Kate's mum." I see her sitting in the middle of the room, my daughter, in her uniform, her hair pulled neatly back into a ponytail, and it strikes me how different she is already, after only a week. "Hello, darling." Her eyes are wide, her mouth parted. She glances down at her desk and goes to close her textbook, then changes her mind and leaves it open, looking to her teacher for direction.

"Katherine, you'd better..."

A girl next to her is packing up Kate's things, as if she is the only person who understands why I'm here. She hands Kate her bag and tries to catch her eye, but my daughter won't lift her head. It was unthinking of me to have chosen a classroom; I should have found her at lunch or in her dormitory. But there isn't anything to be done about that now. I put my arm around her shoulders and take her bag from her as we walk out the door.

She sits quietly on her bed while I put her clothes in the suitcase. The other side of the cubicle is plastered with photos, but Kate has left her own walls bare, confirmation surely that she never really wanted to be here. She doesn't help me pack until I open the top drawer of her bedside table. "I'll do that," she says, as she sweeps the contents quickly into her knapsack, making me wonder what sort of grown-up secrets she has learnt so quickly to harbor.

It is easy to take her. I had expected the young history teacher to alert someone. But no one stops us as we traipse down the stairs of the girls' dorms with her suitcase and bedcovers. For the first hour of the journey, I find myself looking in the mirror, as if the school might have called the gardaí, but I catch myself and laugh. Why would they do that? Kate is mine.

She sleeps most of the journey, wrapped in her duvet in the backseat. As we pass through the checkpoint in the North, she wakes briefly when the soldiers peer into the car. They grin at her, the pattern from the seats tattooed into her flushed cheeks. When we're over the border, she rummages around in the plastic bag at her feet and takes out the sandwiches I've brought.

"Which one do you want?" she asks.

"You choose." She feeds me bites, watching the road in front carefully so that she doesn't distract me at a dangerous moment, but the car bumps over the cat's-eyes anyway. Pulling the sandwich back, she says, "Be careful, Mum."

She falls asleep again, waking only with the thundering of the cattle grid as we cross the threshold between world and home.

The cottage is cold and dark. Kate sits on her bed and chatters her teeth dramatically. "Where's Dad?"

"I don't know."

"Did he not know I was coming home?"

When I don't answer, she says, "It's freezing in here."

"Why not put the kettle on, then?"

I go into the bathroom. Cold air leaks in under the door. He must be back. I wash my hands quickly. But it's Mrs. Connolly. I pause, unseen, at the threshold of the kitchen.

She asks, "Are you sick, *alannah?*"

"No."

"So what is it that brings you home?"

There is silence and I wonder what sort of messages are passing between them. I wait for Mrs. Connolly to leave before I go in. There is a plate on the table with scones covered in cling film.

"Did she bring those?" I ask, as I slide them into the bin. We take our tea into Kate's bedroom. She has managed to pilfer a scone; she gnaws a butterless, jamless corner.

"May I open it?" I kneel down in front of her suitcase, mindful of her new grown-upness. She puts the scone down and opens it herself. Taking out a pile of jeans and t-shirts, she moves towards her chest of drawers. There is no end to how dutiful this child is today. That place has already made her submissive.

"Not your own clothes. You can leave them in." I reach inside and pull out her uniform, her school shoes. "Just these." I hang them up in her wardrobe.

"What are you doing, Mum?"

"You'll see in a sec. Finish your tea."

She puts her empty teacup down with a flourish, as if to say, *Okay, I'm ready.*

I close her suitcase and turn it onto its wheels. As we leave, I see Francis watching television in the front room of their cottage. Mary will be busy in the kitchen at the back, making dinner. The Connollys don't eat the leftovers from the restaurant; it's not their sort of thing.

The big house is quiet. I pull the letter I've written to John out of my pocket and leave it on the hall table. It occurs to me for the first time that he might be in his study; I forgot to ask what his plans were for the day. Did he even notice I was gone? On the stairs, I listen for a late tour group. We haven't far to go, but it wouldn't do to run into them. I put Kate's suitcase down and pull my shoes off. I gesture that she should do the same. If she was sorry to have been taken out of school, she hasn't complained. If she misses her new friends, she hasn't said a word. And now, as I lead her away again from what she is used to, she follows. At the end of the landing, I pull the key out of my pocket and open the door to the third floor.

When I have safely locked it behind us, Kate says, "I thought we weren't allowed up here."

"Philip the First intended this to be the ballroom, you know."

"I know, Mum."

"It's very unusual to have a ballroom at the top of a house."

Kate considers this. "Why wasn't it a ballroom in the end?"

"Philip the First thought God wouldn't approve. He was a Presbyterian. Presbyterians don't approve of dancing."

"Why?"

"Because they don't like to have too much fun." And then I felt badly for not giving her a proper answer. "To be honest, I'm not sure; it might be because they associate dances with drinking and they don't drink, or it might be because they think that dancing might lead to sex and they don't approve of that either. Or it might be a little of both."

"Oh."

John would disapprove of me talking to her about sex, but she's nearly thirteen. It's about time, and she would have learnt about it in that school sooner rather than later. He probably hadn't thought of that.

We rest at the top of the stairs. I am proud of the work I've done. It will be heaven to wake up here after the darkness of the cottage. I throw open the curtains I've made so that the light will stream in tomorrow morning. The movement catches the eye of a groundsman below. He looks up but, thinking he's mistaken, moves away, grinding a cigarette into the gravel. When I turn, Kate is at the far end of the room, staring at the painting covering the end wall.

"Do you recognize what it is? It's called a trompe l'oeil."

She moves a few steps closer. It's Dulough: lake, forest, hills, hanging valleys, the cirque at the end, even the Connollys' cottage, small and white, with a plume of smoke curling its way to the heavens. The sky is dark, and clouds roll in from the sea, so real that one can feel the threat of rain. The deer herd is at the edge of the forest and there are wood pigeons in the trees. There is the island and the church, the stained glass window still intact. There is the side avenue and the road to town, and there is the house, dark, overgrown with ivy, its turrets shooting into the wet sky. The whole thing could move at any moment; the deer go into the forest, the rain begins, Mrs. Connolly comes out of her cottage to take in the washing. Kate traces her finger along the edge of the lake; when she takes it away it is stained blue.

"An artist called Geoffrey Roe did this. More than a hundred years ago. Do you like it?"

Kate nods.

I am suddenly happy. I take her hand. "Come on, I'll teach you how to waltz."

She reluctantly allows herself to be led in small dancing circles, her feet dragging on the floor, her arms limp.

"Stand up straight." I hum my own made-up tune. "That's it, you're not bad at all."

We move about the vast room. I hold my one remaining child closer and closer and when I forget to sing, we lose the rhythm of our steps. Soon our dance is only a series of hushed lurches left and right, backwards and forwards, until we stop altogether and stand in the middle of the room, still.

THE SPRING AFTER

John has been monastic this winter, speech kept to a bare minimum, usually with Murphy or Mrs. Connolly, and only about the business of opening the estate again for the upcoming season. Marianne is to come home today. She has been in Dublin all winter, where her parents have been looking after her, careful not to make promises about when she might be ready to return to Donegal. Though John has not admitted it to himself until now, he has worried that she might not come back, that she might choose to stay in the city. He has come out to the island for a last morning of solitude, to ready himself for her return. Sitting on the wreckage of the fallen church, he has a view of Philip's grave and of the hut his son had just finished building when he died.

Marianne's parents have discouraged John from speaking to her whilst she's been away. When they do talk, he is careful about the subjects he chooses: her garden, Kate. His wife seems to have accepted that their daughter will stay at boarding school now, where she is happy. Kate has asked if she might bring a friend home for the Easter holidays, which they have taken as a good sign.

The night Marianne was forced down from the ballroom, after John carried her downstairs into the watery winter light, slipping her into the back of her parents' car, Kate had slept on the floor of his bedroom. He hadn't known what to say to her, so he offered to read her stories, as he had when she was little. She fetched a stack of books, and he read for more than two hours, his voice growing hoarse towards the end, willing her to sleep. But he had been prepared to read all night if that's what was needed.

For the next few days, they had drifted around the cottage. Kate spent most of her time curled up, reading on her bed, not the books she'd asked him to read that first night, but more grown-up books, with the stamp of the boarding school library on them. John hoped she was trying to keep up with her English class. He was afraid to leave her alone in the cottage, but he longed for his study, where he'd be able to think properly.

On the third day, he had brought Kate into town for lunch. It was a mistake; people stared at them. It was certainly common knowledge what had happened to Philip, but John wondered whether they knew that Marianne had locked herself and Kate in the ballroom and that the police had paid a visit to Dulough. The Connollys wouldn't have said anything, but it was possible that one of the gardaí had. He finished his food quickly and called for the bill as Kate was beginning the second half of her sandwich.

It was strange bringing her back to Dublin the following Sunday, the boot full of her things, her duvet across the backseat, everything exactly as it was when he'd driven her down the first time. Then, it was the end of the summer, the hedgerows still full of flowers, green after a wet August. When he brought her back the second time, it was the middle of October, and the early snowfall had dulled the countryside. She seemed more nervous than on the first trip; she chewed her fingernails, a new habit, and one he didn't much like. He tried to make conversation, about friends she was looking forward to seeing again, about whether she would play hockey, about which teachers she liked, but her answers were monosyllabic. It was not behavior his father would have allowed of John when he was the same age.

When they got to the outskirts of Dublin, she spoke for the first time. "Can I go and see Mum this weekend?"

He hoped Kate hadn't agreed to go back to school only to heighten the possibility of seeing her mother, because he wasn't at all sure that Marianne would be well enough. He could phone his parents-in-law to ask, but he hadn't heard from them in the week since they'd taken Marianne, other than a text message from Patrick to say that they had arrived safely after the journey and to try not to worry. John had seen finality in this, a clear message from Patrick and Anna that he should leave their daughter alone for the time being.

"I don't think this weekend, no," he told Kate.

She turned away from the window, towards him.

"I think Mum might need a little time to herself," he said gently. "I'm sure it won't be too long."

When they pulled up in front of the dorms, a girl with black hair tied into a neat ponytail came out to meet them. She had obviously been waiting for Kate; he prayed it was her own idea and not the school's—that his daughter would have at least one good friend here. As he heaved out her duvet and then opened the boot, the house mistress approached. John tried to remember her name as she gave Kate a hug. She smiled at John and took the duvet from him in a manner that suggested that he wasn't invited into the girls' dorms now that the semester was in full swing.

"All right," he said to Kate, and kissed her awkwardly on the top of her head.

"Bye, Dad," she said, as he got into the car.

She waved until he was out of sight. It was obvious that she was glad to be back. As he drove away from the school, he'd felt relieved, but when he reached Dulough's gates, he found tears were on his cheeks. He wondered how long they'd been there.

There is no housework for him to do in preparation for Marianne's return. Though it's certainly not her job anymore, Mrs. Connolly has made the cottage spick-and-span. He tried to help. He is now adept at washing; he no longer forgets to take in the clothes from the line before they're whipped away by the wind and go tumbling through the gorse. And he knows how to make himself a decent cooked breakfast. Simple stuff. He understands this, but these tasks fell to Marianne when they moved. It was no longer Mrs. Connolly's duty to cook and clean for them. And John hadn't thought to help his wife.

In the ballroom, Marianne had her own private housekeeping. He went up to dismantle their things the day after he returned Kate to school. Mrs. Connolly offered to help, but he had demurred; Marianne wouldn't have liked it. She wouldn't have wanted Mrs. Connolly to have such intimate contact with the life she'd created for herself and Kate. When Marianne first

arrived at Dulough, she had hated that Mrs. Connolly went into
their room, made their bed, put their clothes away. Their first ar-
gument as a married couple was when she insisted that he stop
this practice, that Mrs. Connolly would clean the common ar-
eas of the big house, but that she, Marianne, would make their
bed—and later the children's beds—and take care of washing
and ironing the family's clothes. As he opened the door to the
ballroom, he thought he could understand the intimacy of possessions. The moving men had made him feel something of what
Marianne had felt in those early days.

He climbed the rough wooden stairs and passed through the
space where the second door was before the policeman had demanded that it be taken off its hinges. The air was fresher than it
had been a few weeks earlier. He wondered how this was possible; none of the windows opened. It mustn't have been terribly
good for them, all those days of stale air, he thought. He hoped
it hadn't done Kate any damage.

John had never been in the ballroom before the day they'd
rescued Kate. He'd barely registered its existence, barely ever
thought of it. The door had always been locked and he had always known that the key was in the safe. He and his brother
had been told that the floors were unfinished, dangerous, but
John was astonished to see that the room was much more complete than he had been led to believe, that there was a stairs one
could climb quite easily, that there were two beautiful marble
fireplaces. Marianne had been able to make them quite a comfortable apartment up there.

As he paused to get his breath at the top of the stairs, he was
confronted with the painting on the end wall. It was Dulough itself, the house in the foreground, taller, much more gothic than

in real life but a very close likeness. He bent down to look at the signature in the corner: Geoffrey Roe.

Over the front door, the rose was in bloom, but it didn't climb as it did now. He looked more closely at the painting: Everything was newer, sharper, younger. It wasn't just the house; the trees in the forest and at the foot of the garden were still in their infancy, the gardens newly laid out, the original flower bed designs clear, as if they'd just been lifted from the paper on which they'd been drawn. All that remained unchanged was the landscape; the hills were still steep and tall, precisely the same as they were today when he looked out the window in his study, and the lake was as black as he'd ever seen it. Like the scale of the house, the lake's had been altered; it was larger than it was in real life. He noticed the same obsession with water he'd seen in the Water Women exhibit all those years earlier. The bath in which Olivia Campbell lay had also been elongated and brimming to the point of spilling over, so as to give Roe the opportunity to lavish attention on his presentation of the water itself.

John's eyes traveled left, to the very edge of the trompe l'oeil, to the sea and to the island on which the church stood, the stained glass window still intact. Here, too, Roe had painted the water as brimming around the island, much further up the rocks than it went in reality. The whole painting gave the impression that Dulough might be engulfed at any moment, the lake rising to envelop the house, the sea covering the island, the land reclaimed, the work of his ancestor obliterated.

He made his way to the far end of the room and pulled the sheets off the bed. They were sour. He would wash them himself rather than allowing Mrs. Connolly to do it; that would please Marianne. He opened a chest that he recognized as having come from Philip's old room. Inside, Kate's and Marianne's clothes were folded neatly; he took them out and put them in piles on the bed. At the bottom of the trunk, he came across some of Philip's clothes, a green woolen jumper and blue corduroy trousers. A pair of shoes with the socks tucked neatly inside lay underneath. John sat down on the mattress with Philip's clothes in his arms. He told himself that it wasn't very strange, that all his things were still hanging in his cupboard in the cottage—neither he nor Marianne had made any move to change that. But he was disturbed at finding them here, the deliberateness of Marianne's having chosen them and brought them up with her own things. Had Kate seen them? He hoped not.

On the writing desk, his daughter's textbooks were lined up in alphabetical order, her copybooks stacked neatly, with each subject printed clearly on the front. He should have thought to bring these down with them to Dublin when he returned her to school yesterday. They would probably put a whole new set of textbooks on his bill, as well as the extra tutelage. He sat at the desk, knees knocking against the top, and opened Kate's geography copybook. He had been heartened by the fact that Marianne was making sure that Kate did schoolwork, but he realized that much of it was work he'd already finished with the children a year ago. He leafed through Kate's work. There was a drawing tucked into the back; it was the picture of the valley that Philip had done just after the move. John had returned to the cottage from a meeting with Foyle to find Philip upset about Marianne's reaction to the gardeners digging up the lawn. John remembers his own anger at his wife for worrying about the garden rather than her son that afternoon.

In the ballroom, he looked at the geography book, at Kate's

copybook, at Philip's drawing lined up side by side; why had Marianne been repeating work she knew the children had already done?

He worked late into the night; it was eleven o'clock before he dragged the last piece of furniture—Kate's desk—down the stairs, returning it to the little bedroom at the end of the landing. He went back up to the ballroom with a torch to take a last look around; it looked exactly as it must have when Marianne first opened it up. He shone the light over Geoffrey Roe's painting one last time; he was very sorry to leave this behind. Why had his parents never shown it to him? Had they known it was here? He wouldn't tell Frank Foyle or Mr. Murphy about it; Roe was quite famous these days, and no doubt they would want visitors to be able to see it. But John wasn't prepared to have strangers up here. He would keep the secret of the painting for him and for Marianne. Anyway, he told himself, he could come up and look at it any time he wanted; he was the one with the key.

When John got old, he hoped he would lose his memory, as his mother did, her mind like a cave disintegrating, powder falling from the ceiling cracks, water washing in at its mouth. He would forget the past year; he would be buried on the island. In a thousand years, Dulough wouldn't exist anyway; it would be seed and memories of seed. Perhaps there would be another ice age. That would certainly have pleased Philip.

The day that Mrs. Connolly phoned him at college to tell him that his mother was dying, John came back from the city as fast as he could, but it was too late. She was upstairs, laid out on her bed, looking for all the world as if she might open her eyes and ask for some tea. They tried to bury her a couple days later.

Three men from the funeral home in town arrived to help carry the coffin out to the island, just as they had for Philip's funeral. But John had miscalculated the tides; when they got down to the beach, sea still surrounded the island. It had already been difficult getting down the cliff path; John, who was carrying the front of his mother's coffin, his left arm extended to grip his brother's shoulder, had felt the weight inside shift as they made their way down the steep path. He could tell that even the smallest amount of water lapping at their ankles could unbalance them, and so he announced that they should turn back and wait. He avoided the men as Mrs. Connolly fed them around the kitchen table, though they were probably very glad of her cooking. Phil went up to his old bedroom in disgust, a man of the city with no time for mistakes such as this.

John had sat in the upstairs drawing room window for a couple of hours, squinting at the island, watching for the last of the sea to be sucked out and hidden behind it before he went down to the kitchen to fetch the men for a second attempt. One of them joked quietly that it was as well they'd had a trial run anyway, with the way down to the beach being so steep. But John knew that was nothing compared to the rocks at the foot of the island, which they would have to maneuver his mother across slowly. If the tide came back in too soon they'd all be there for the night. Afterwards, he tried to convince Francis that the grave could wait to be filled until the next morning, when it was properly light again. His mother wouldn't have wanted Francis to risk being stranded. He gave a nod and turned away, but John knew that he didn't think he was much of a son to leave his mother's coffin down there, covered for the night with nothing but an old piece of plywood and some plastic sheeting.

Phil had done nothing to help prepare for their mother's funeral. He treated the three days after she died as if they were a test of his forbearance. He wouldn't take responsibility for the notice in the paper or for phoning relatives. What it was exactly about Dulough that Phil couldn't stand eluded John, but it was clear that not even their mother's death could change these feelings. Phil remained in his room except at mealtimes and muttered *work* under his breath when he disappeared again after pudding.

A few years earlier, when Phil had taken a job at a law practice in Dublin, their mother had called him and then John into the drawing room one evening after Christmas, the only time Phil came home. His mother hadn't said what passed between her and John's elder brother that allowed her to announce that the estate would go to John, but it didn't come as a surprise. In many ways, Phil's behavior during the days between her death and funeral was an extreme version of the way that he had been behaving for a long time, first as a teenager, then as a student. Everything about him was at odds with Dulough: his impatience, his disdain for nature, his interest in money. John supposed that it had been clear to his parents from quite early on that Phil was much more like Olivia's son, Duncan, who'd eschewed his father's Irish estate in favor of setting up a legal practice in Edinburgh. And so John's mother did what Olivia had done and left the estate to someone who really wanted it.

Until the moment his mother had told him that she was going to will Dulough to him, John had never doubted that he did want to live there. But when he closed the door to the drawing room and went upstairs to think about it, it hit him for the first time that he might not want the estate after all. He had yet to

meet Marianne—in fact he had never had a successful relationship. Girls at Trinity showed interest in him, but they always fell
away after an evening in the pub or a drawn-out coffee. He had
a growing sense of unease that there was something wrong with
him, but he hadn't been able to work out quite what it was. His
clothes seemed the most likely possibility and so he'd bought
himself a new wardrobe and then discarded it when a girl in
one of his lectures told him that she liked him better the other
way. He hadn't, then, wondered what deeper deficiencies he had
that might stop people from falling in love with him, deficiencies Marianne had made him well aware of since.

The night his mother told him he would inherit Dulough, he
worried that he wouldn't find someone who wanted to live here
with him. He considered going back downstairs to tell her he'd
changed his mind, but then who would take care of the place?
A cousin somewhere? Or, worse, would it be sold? The thought
of either had made him feel so sick that he had decided that,
whether he found someone who wanted to be here with him or
not, he would come back after college and do his best by the estate. Then he'd met Marianne.

"Try not to look so happy. It's embarrassing," she said teasingly when she accepted his marriage proposal.

It was true that he hadn't been able to believe his luck; not
only had she agreed to marry him, she had agreed to live at
Dulough. As they drove back to Donegal after the proposal, he
thought he'd better start educating her about the area, so he told
her that in Irish the Poison Glen was really the Heavenly Glen,
but when the English were mapping the country and appropriating Irish names to suit their own tongues, they made a mistake, there being only two letters' difference between "heaven"

and "poison" in Irish. But he had yet to tell her of what Philip the First had done, that he'd thrown his tenants off the land right after the Famine, without a care as to what happened to them.

They drove through the gates and up the avenue, the lake on their right, the valley closing in to the sea on both sides. He parked the car in front of the house. Mrs. Connolly came out to meet them as she had the first time he'd brought Marianne. She embraced his fiancée warmly. John was relieved; he hadn't been sure how Mrs. Connolly would take to the future Mrs. Campbell; she had been devoted to the last one.

Francis helped take their bags upstairs. John could see him stealing glances at Marianne, sizing her up. She was beautiful, after all, there was no way around that, but John knew that Francis was looking for something beyond beauty in a woman who would live at Dulough. Mrs. Connolly led the way to his parents' old bedroom, instead of that of his childhood, confirming him only then as the true owner of the estate in her eyes.

After Francis and Mary retreated, Marianne disappeared into the little bathroom adjoining their bedroom, a luxury his mother had added in her later years. When she emerged, though she hadn't changed clothes, her countenance told him that she had made the decision to cast off her student self, that she was ready to become mistress of Dulough. He put his arm through hers as they went down to dinner.

There had been no mishaps at Philip's funeral as there had been at John's mother's. Marianne put herself in charge of everything. They were fortunate. The Atlantic dragged itself further out than he'd ever seen it, giving them more than enough time to make their way across the sand and to hold a half-hour-long service of sorts; none of the Campbells had been religious since Philip the First. Kate read part of *The Wind in the Willows* beautifully, clearly, as her feet sank into the mound of earth next to the grave, which John had chosen to be as close as possible to Philip's hut.

Though Marianne had been the first to suspect that Philip was making secret trips to the island, John had been the one to discover what Philip had been building. On the day after Philip drowned, Mr. Flanagan, the funeral director in town, asked whether they should send some men to dig the grave. John said that there was no need, that Francis would do it. Then he'd caught himself in his cruelty.

"We'll send a few men tomorrow," said Mr. Flanagan. "You'll just need to let them know where."

So John was forced to go out to the island to decide where Philip should be buried. He wandered amongst the stones of his ancestors, thinking that perhaps it was time to break this Campbell tradition; he couldn't bear the thought of his son out here alone. As he scanned the island, a little structure at the far end of the graveyard had caught his eye. When he got closer, he could see that it was a hut and that it had been built out of the drystone walls. The roof was made of planks of wood that stuck out the front to make a little porch. Francis had asked John if the men from the government had been given permission to take wood from the barn; he'd noticed bits and pieces going missing. John had said he'd talk to Mr. Murphy about it, but he'd known that he couldn't do anything, that the government men could take whatever they wanted. John should have realized where the wood had gone.

As he neared the hut, he heard the crash of waves at the

end of the island and the sea wind loud in his ears. He fixed his eyes on the opening, half believing that Philip might crawl out, grinning at the trick he'd played on all of them. But John himself had taken Philip's wet body out of Francis's arms the previous evening and laid him on the new couch in the drawing room, as Marianne watched, ashen. John had tried to remember what he'd learnt in school, tilting Philip's head back, opening the mouth, checking to see if there was anything obstructing the airway—seaweed, perhaps—but there wasn't. He breathed into his son's lungs, watching the little chest rise with his own breath, so like real breath. Then, two firm hands on his shoulders, moving him out of the way: a German doctor on holiday in Donegal. John stood back, next to Marianne, looking on, as the doctor pressed on Philip's body much more roughly than seemed right. John took a step forwards to stop him, but Francis gripped his arm firmly. The doctor turned to them, the palms of his hands turned upwards in a gesture of helplessness or apology, and Marianne said: "Kate." Mrs. Connolly turned and went out at that moment, as if the word were a command directed at her.

John had got down on his hands and knees and crawled inside the hut; it was dark, the walls had been well made, the holes between the big stones filled with little ones and filled again with mud. It was warm too, completely sheltered from the wind. In the corner was an old biscuit tin. He opened it. Inside was one of John's books from when he was a child, *Five Get into a Fix*. Under it was a bar of chocolate, half gone, and the small torch Philip had been given in his stocking the previous Christmas. John switched it on and shone it up at the ceiling, where a long-legged spider went about its business. Pulling his knees up to his chest, he rested his head between them. When he left the hut hours later, he went to the nearest point in the graveyard and made an outline in stones so that the men would know exactly where to dig.

John had meant to give the tin with the book and the chocolate and the torch to Mr. Flanagan to be put in Philip's coffin, but he'd changed his mind at the last minute and kept it for himself. He wouldn't show it to Marianne; the presence of the Famous Five book seemed to make him somehow more culpable, which was stupid, he thought later, because he couldn't have been any more culpable. Marianne had pointed this fact out in the letter she'd left for him when she retreated to the ballroom with Kate.

John,

Before I met you, I would have said that families with a history like yours deserved to lose everything, and so I was surprised when I fell in love with you. I was even more surprised when I fell in love with Dulough. I can see now that that's why you didn't tell me we were in trouble; you couldn't bear to disappoint me. But there shouldn't be secrets between husbands and wives.

I found Olivia's diaries while you were in Dublin leaving Kate at that school. I read all of them, from beginning to end. I probably know them better than you do now. Then I did a little research of my own, at the new Internet café in town. First I just wanted to understand more about Geoffrey Roe and Olivia. There was nothing there about them, although I did find out he wasn't as wild as she—or Philip the First—imagined. It was another painter who started the rumour that he had been littering the British Empire with his offspring. In fact, there's no mention of him ever having gone to Africa, or doing much trav-

elling at all really. It's entirely possible that Donegal was the most exotic place he'd ever been. He wouldn't be the first man to make himself sound more interesting than he actually was.

I couldn't tear myself away from the computer, so I paid for another hour; I wanted to know more about that ancestor of yours, the man who gave our son his name. It's all there: the evictions, what happened to the families afterwards (the poorhouse or the boat to Australia, if you're interested), the scholarships Olivia set up at the local school, which even she knew did nothing to make amends for what her husband had done, her obituary. There was of course no mention anywhere of Dulough during the Civil War. Nothing. When I got home, I found Francis in the gardens. The poor thing looked so nervous when I approached him, and I'll tell you that I was fairly nervous myself; it's no easy thing to remind people around here of your family's history. He must have thought I was going to talk about the day he found Philip. When he realised that wasn't what I was after, he relaxed. I asked whether it was true what you wrote about the IRA occupying Dulough. He told me it wasn't. Do you realise that you've lost the Connollys with that? Did you think what he and Mary would make of you? You didn't, did you? I'm sure Murphy loved that stuff, though. Well done, it'll certainly bring more money in....

There was more, but John didn't like to think about the rest. It listed the various ways he'd disappointed her since they got married, how he'd let her down, how he'd let his family down. Other than the fact that Marianne had done research into Dulough's history, what she said in her letter didn't come as much of a surprise. It was simply a gathering together of many things she'd already intimated. It was funny how those small intimations held so much less weight separately than they did when they were all strung together as they were in her letter, lined up like soldiers in a firing squad. Even the fact that she'd found out he'd lied in the brochure wasn't much of a surprise; it was only how she found out. She had been more intrepid than he expected. He had thought it more likely that Phil would mention sometime that so much of the brochure was made up—not so much as a revelation, but as an acknowledgment that for once in his life John had shown some business acumen.

But it was the last line of the letter that had troubled John most at the time: *You don't need to worry about us. We'll be perfectly comfortable. You have your study. Kate and I need somewhere, too.*

He couldn't think what she was talking about. As far as he knew, Kate was in school and Marianne had spent the day in her garden. When had he seen her last? That morning? No. She had taken to sleeping in Kate's bed, leaving him alone in their new room; she had been up long before him. He hadn't said anything about this sleeping arrangement; it was the way he found things when he got back from dropping Kate at school. He thought that when she got used to Kate being away, she would come back.

He went to the cottage. The lights were off, but her car was there. Perhaps she'd left him a message on the kitchen table as she often did, but before he got to the kitchen, he noticed the answering machine blinking; it was the principal of Kate's school, a supercilious man named Robert Goodman.

"Mr. and Mrs. Campbell, I'm phoning to inform you that it is against school policy for parents to remove children from class unless it's an emergency situation. I very much hope this wasn't the case today. I await your phone call."

John's first thought was that the principal had it wrong; how could Marianne have gone to Dublin without him realizing? He circled the cottage, throwing open doors, turning on lights; there was no one there, but something in Kate's room caught his eye. Her wardrobe was open and inside he could see her two school uniforms hanging there. Underneath, her new school shoes were lined up next to the pile of bags from the shopping trip she and Marianne had taken in August. He went next door. Francis and Mary were eating dinner.

"Terribly sorry to bother you...I don't suppose you've seen Marianne?"

Mrs. Connolly rose from the table. "Are they not in there?" She inclined her head in the direction of his cottage. Then, reading his expression, she said, "Did you not know Kate was coming home?"

Francis, who'd been watching silently, set his knife and fork down beside his plate and began pulling on his coat.

When John and Francis got to the house, it was as dark as John had left it half an hour earlier. He couldn't see how his wife and daughter could be inside, but Francis began turning on the lights in every room. The drawing room looked the same as it had for the past few months, the blue ropes hanging on brass poles. The only difference between this room and the one conceived of by Murphy was that the couch had been replaced after Francis had brought Philip in from the sea, kicking the ropes out of the way, laying the wet child gently down. John wondered briefly whether Francis noticed that the couch had been changed.

In the hall, John called out his wife's, then his daughter's, name, still convinced of the futility of looking for them there.

"They won't be in the kitchen," Francis said. "Mary would have seen them before she came down."

Francis began to ascend the stairs. John followed. He noticed that Francis didn't call their names; even at a moment like this, it would have seemed presumptuous. On the landing, the older man paused, turning his head left and right. There were no lights on in any of the bedrooms; that much was obvious. They could see under every door from their vantage point at the top of the staircase, and both of them knew Marianne well enough to understand that she wouldn't stay in a room with a light off, not on her own, and certainly not with Kate. John was getting frustrated; why couldn't Francis see they weren't there? They must be outside somewhere—it wasn't completely dark yet. He wanted to find Marianne as soon as possible, to know what she was playing at, why she'd taken Kate out of school without consulting him first. He turned to go back downstairs, but Francis grabbed him by the sleeve and inclined his head heavenward.

"Up there," he said.

John thought for a moment that the old man, usually so rational and resolute, was losing his grip on reality.

"What do you mean?"

"They're up in that ballroom."

John led the way to the study, where he searched the safe for the key. At the door to the ballroom, John knocked first quietly, then loudly. He still didn't quite believe that his wife and daughter were on the other side. Francis stood back.

Kate came as soon as he knocked.

"Dad?"

He tried to glean whether she sounded afraid, but the wood muffled her voice.

"Is Mum there?"

Then he heard a floorboard creak; it was Marianne, telling their daughter to go back to bed. John tried to talk to her, to get her to open the door, but Francis shook his head. Francis and Marianne often spent hours in the gardens together, bent over one plant or another; perhaps the older man knew her better than John had realized. Francis whispered that it was best to leave them alone for the moment.

After John asked Kate whether she was hungry and reassured her that they'd be back in the morning, the two men went to the Connollys' cottage, where John allowed Francis to explain to Mrs. Connolly what had happened. John could see that Mrs. Connolly didn't approve of leaving Kate up there for the night, but she always deferred to her husband's judgment. She agreed to make Marianne and Kate a breakfast tray the next morning whilst John worked out what to do.

The following day, when John brought up the meal that Mrs. Connolly had prepared for them, he watched, hidden behind a pillar at the top of the stairs, as Marianne, still in her long nightgown, opened the door. What had he been planning to do, he wondered, as she stooped to pick up the tray—grab it from her, force his way in? He couldn't allow Kate to see something so upsetting, and so he'd stayed quiet, thinking that the only thing to do was acquiesce until Marianne came to her senses. After three meals, Mrs. Connolly seemed to accept that this was how things had to be for the time being. She began to prepare the trays without being asked.

It was because of the lucidity of Marianne's letter that John gave no thought to whether his wife had changed from being the woman he'd always known to someone else, someone who wasn't to be trusted with their remaining child. Because he himself had needed to keep his study, because as soon as he'd seen Philip's hut, he'd recognized the same impulse in his son, there had been no more logical statement than Marianne's that she needed somewhere too. And because Marianne had always known what was best for the children, he assumed she knew what was best for Kate now, that he had been wrong about the school, and that Marianne was righting the damage he had done to Kate. In fact, in their first few weeks in the ballroom, John was much more concerned with concealing what was going on from Bríd, the tour guide, and from Mr. Murphy. Fortunately, the tours were tapering away, the summer season over. When the house closed in mid-September for the winter, John was relieved.

But one morning, after a heavy frost, he discovered an uneaten breakfast tray outside the door to the ballroom. It was the first time that the food Mrs. Connolly had prepared hadn't been eaten. He knocked, but there was no answer, so he picked up the tray and brought it back to the kitchen. He waited until he heard Mrs. Connolly go into the scullery, and then he quickly dumped the contents into the bin, covering it with other scraps. If the old woman found out that Kate had missed a meal she'd be very worried. In the weeks since his wife and daughter had retreated to the ballroom, Mrs. Connolly had said little about the new arrangement, but he knew that as the husband and, moreover, as the owner of Dulough, she thought he should put his foot down. *Enough of this nonsense* was what she was thinking.

That lunchtime, he hovered outside the kitchen. When she emerged with the lunch tray, he swooped out of the shadows of the passageway, scaring her to the point of almost dropping it.

"I'll take that up today, thank you, Mrs. Connolly." When he got to the door to the ballroom, he laid the tray on the ground and rapped on the door. "There's your lunch," he said, loudly. He wanted Marianne to know that it wasn't Mrs. Connolly who'd brought it but him, and that he would notice if it wasn't eaten. But Marianne had never been the slightest bit afraid of him.

Then he sat in his study, chair swiveled towards the valley, frost covering the land all the way down to the lake. The lake itself was darker than he'd ever seen it, as if it was deepening as the years went by, the bottom falling away and away. One night, when they were still in the big house, they had woken to cries coming from Philip's bedroom. He and Marianne ran down the corridor and into their son's room. The cries were coming from his sleep. Marianne sat down by Philip's bed and gently rubbed his arm until he stopped. When she was satisfied that the nightmare was over, she led John back to bed, but he wasn't able to sleep. What sort of terror had gripped Philip? John never remembered having dreams like that himself. When Marianne was asleep again, he had slipped out of their bed and returned to his son's room. He sat in the chair in the corner, his dressing gown over him as a blanket, watching Philip's sleeping form.

When he woke in the morning, Philip was standing next to him in his striped pajamas, looking bewildered. John took him on his lap and asked if he remembered what he had dreamt about. The lake, Philip had said, a monster. John looked away. He had been the one to tell him about the Loch Ness Monster a few days previously, and to show him those grainy photos of a tiny dinosaurlike head poking out of the cold waters of the bottomless lake. John had explained to Philip at the time that it was in Scotland and that there were no monsters in their own lake, and though he had seen that Philip had understood, his little imagination must have conflated the two lakes as he slept. The guilt John had felt lasted for a long time. Marianne would never have made such a mistake.

He wondered whether Philip had been scared of what was in the water on the day he died. Both he and Marianne had been keen to ensure that their children weren't afraid of the sea. They had taught Kate and Philip to swim at a young age, to reassure them that there was nothing in their Atlantic to harm them, that there were plenty of creatures to love: crabs, starfish, mussels, limpets. But perhaps they should have instilled a fear of the water into their children. To John's knowledge they had never explained what an undertow was, they had never warned Kate and Philip that the water could suck you down, could suck even grown-up swimmers down.

Until then, John had not allowed himself to think about the end of his son's life. Philip had rolled up his trousers, so he must have thought that he would be able to wade to the island. It would have been very cold, the sea still wintry. He imagined him, eyes fixed on the island, wading forwards with determination. Had the point come when Philip knew that he wouldn't make it? What had it been like to feel the pull of the current, a current that John and Marianne had made sure the children had never experienced? John realized that he himself had no idea, even after all the years of sea-bathing, what a strong undertow felt like. He hoped that Philip hadn't known what was happening, that he believed to the last second that he was going to get to the island, where he would be able to hide in his hut until the strangers had left Dulough.

He couldn't stand to think about it anymore, so he'd gone to see whether Kate and Marianne had eaten their lunch. Surely they would be starving after having missed breakfast. But when he got to the ballroom door, he found their tray again untouched. He knocked loudly.

Kate came to the other side.

"Enough," he said.

He heard Kate's footsteps disappear back into the vast space. A few moments of silence, then a sound that he first thought was coming from somewhere else in the house, below him, Mrs. Connolly hoovering, perhaps. A wave of irritation passed over him that he couldn't hear properly what was happening on the other side of the door. Then he realized, as the sound got louder, that it was a human sound.

Kate returned.

"What's that?" he asked, alarmed.

"It's Mum."

It was the only moment in his life that John remembered having lost control. He bent down and picked up first one bowl of soup, then another, and hurled them at the door, then the plates, the sandwiches, hitting the door, sliding down revoltingly. Everything lay in a pile: broken crockery, food, milk, coffee, soup. The next thing he knew, he was sitting in the kitchen, with Mrs. Connolly cleaning his cuts and mopping at the splatters on his clothes, and he was looking up at her, hands outstretched, as he often had as a child when he'd fallen or fought with his brother.

As soon as she was finished, he had gone to the phone in the hall, though he wasn't supposed to use it anymore, and dialed his parents-in-law's number in Dublin. Marianne's mother answered.

"Anna," he said. For an awful moment, he thought he was going to cry. He took a breath.

"John?"

"Anna, do you think you and Patrick might be able to come up?"

"Why?" He heard the panic in her voice and instantly regretted not telling her that Marianne and Kate were all right.

"It's difficult to explain, but Marianne has, well, locked herself away."

"Where? In the house?"

He paused; he had never really thought of the ballroom as part of the house. But he supposed it *was* in the house, as much a part of the house as any other room. That was comforting; it made Marianne and Kate seem less far away than they had, and he wondered whether he'd been too hasty in phoning her.

"Yes. In the ballroom."

"Why?"

She didn't wait for him to answer.

"We'll leave now," she said.

And John wondered, when he put down the phone, what Marianne's mother and father would think of him when they realized that he'd let this happen. But it was only after Marianne was taken away that he fully realized how inept he'd been. How long would he have let it go on, he had asked himself many times since, if others hadn't stepped in and done what needed to be done?

A movement on the headland interrupts his thoughts. He doesn't know how long he's been sitting out here on the island, the cold having made good progress through his bones.

Someone has come to the end of the garden. It's impossible to tell from this distance whether the figure is male or female, but he can see a face, looking out to sea. It must be Francis; Mrs. Connolly wouldn't leave the kitchen for a walk at this hour. He supposes it could be one of the gardeners or the people from the government, but they always travel in packs. He stays completely still, hoping he blends into the darkness of the ruins behind him. The figure turns, vanishing back into the trees.

At any rate, it's time to go. He wants to pick some flowers from Marianne's garden for the kitchen table, so that she'll see them when she gets in. She has insisted on driving back up from Dublin herself, and though he was disappointed that she didn't want him to collect her, he supposes that she wants to prove she's better, that she's ready to return to life on the estate.

He makes his way down the rocks at the foot of the island and over the beach. When he reaches the bottom of the cliff path, someone calls his name. Marianne is walking towards him. "I've been looking for you for ages. The traffic wasn't too bad."

"You're back," he says.

She's already got her gardening clothes on. He thinks about the figure who came to the edge of the cliff, and matches it now to Marianne in her old coat and mud-stained trousers. The pale smear in the distance had been her face, scanning the horizon for his.

Behind her, the house looks exactly as it did before the opening and for a moment he allows himself to believe that the visitors never came, that Philip is still alive, that the year passed uneventfully, the same as all the years that went before.

Acknowledgments

Black Lake is also dedicated to the memory of Joyce Power-Steele (1909–2009) of Portnoo, Co. Donegal.

Those who know Donegal may recognize that Dulough is loosely based on Glenveagh. I hope readers will forgive the liberties I've taken with its history and geography.

I would like to acknowledge the support of the Robert T. Jones Fellowship at the University of St. Andrews in Scotland and the PEO International Peace Scholarship in the United States for financial assistance with my graduate studies at Columbia.

Sincere thanks to my editor at Little, Brown, New York, Laura Tisdel, for her generous attention to this book; to Reagan Arthur; to Fiona Brown, Jin Yu, and the publicity team; to Betsy Uhrig and Janet Byrne in production; and to jacket designer Kapo Ng. At Headline in London, to my editor, Imogen Taylor, and to Frankie Gray, Frances Gough, and all at Tinder Press.

To my agent, Eleanor Jackson, at Dunow, Carlson & Lerner in New York, I'm beyond grateful.

Acknowledgments

Love and thanks to the following teachers, colleagues, and friends: Sarah Adams, Silke Aisenbrey, Elisa Albert, Barbara Blatner, Ruth Bowie, Michael Callaghan, Vanessa Carswell, Amit Chaudhuri, Lucy Faulconbridge, John and Sue Hemingway, Joanne Jacobson, Elizabeth Kadetsky, Binnie Kirshenbaum, Kerri Majors, Rachel Mesch, Caroline Murnane, Els Quaegebeur, Liesl Schwabe, Fred Sugarman, and Josh Weil. And, from a long time ago, Dorothea Finan, Niall MacMonagle, and Alan Gray

But most of all, above all, to my husband, Mike.

About the Author

Johanna Lane grew up in Ireland, studied English literature at the University of St. Andrews in Scotland, and earned her MFA at Columbia University. She lives in New York City.